THE GLASS MOUNTAIN

By W. S. Kuniczak

Novels:
Valedictory
The March
The Thousand Hour Day

Translations:
Quo Vadis (Henryk Sienkiewicz)
"The Trilogy" (Henryk Sienkiewicz)
(I) *With Fire and Sword*
(II) *The Deluge*
(III) *Fire in the Steppe*

History:
My Name is Million

Anthology:
The Glass Mountain

Entertainments:
The Sempinski Affair

THE GLASS MOUNTAIN

Twenty-Six Ancient Polish Folktales and Fables

W. S. Kuniczak

Illustrated by Pat Bargielski

HIPPOCRENE BOOKS
New York

ISBN 0-7818-0087-0

For information, address:
HIPPOCRENE BOOKS, INC.
171 Madison Avenue
New York, NY 10016

Library of Congress Cataloging-in-Publication Data available.

Printed in the United States of America

For Beth, Julie and John Nelson
and their parents

Contents

Introduction

Several years ago Dr. Albert Juszczak, then president of the Kosciuszko Foundation in New York, brought me an anthology of Polish folk tales that sent me tumbling head-over-heels back into my childhood. The year was instantly 1935. I was five years old. I saw my Old Nurse (actually Marysia was a mere 10 years older than I at that time), heard the tales she told me in a far-away, mist-laden corner of Volhynia, lost to Poland through Soviet "liberation" in 1945 and now a part of whatever is emerging from the carcass of the Soviet Union, and a world of memory came back with a rush. Her tales, later given a genteel twist in my mother's admonitory renditions, gave an entirely new interpretation to my reality although that wasn't what mother had in mind. I understood at once that there was more to heaven and hell than any Horatio dreamed of, and that the world of magic and illusion made at least as much sense as any other explanation of the life around me. To this day I merely need to close my eyes to see escapist theater at its best, unfolding in an imaginary picture show and charting the marvelous geography of the fantastic. Some of the tales that Marysia told me are universal in all the Western Slavic languages and cultures and have been told and retold for 1,000 years.

The Glass Mountain is by no means a comprehensive anthology of anybody's folklore. In fact no seminal work of that kind exists. What you see here is at best a sampler of the more than 6,000 Polish and Ruthenian folktales that have been collected in the last 150 years even though some of them go back to the strolling minstrels of the Middle Ages. Its purpose is to stir the imagination and arouse curiosity about this enchanted and enchanting world of simple moral lessons, broad wit, sly allegory and an abiding faith in the betterment of our lot. Written over the years as I remembered the tales and their telling, this small collection is brought together to awaken interest in the much larger whole.

The Polish folk tale evolves from two sources: the troubadour themes entering from the West and the barbaric, earthy currents flowing from the East. But there is no conflict in this innocent collision and that is surely magical in itself. As in so much else that creates the totality of Polish history, literature and culture, the two opposing currents of the East and the West come together smoothly, blending into a homogeneous whole, and creating something far richer and greater than the sum of the parts.

Folktales are the earliest literature known to Man, never meant to be set down on paper. They represent a pure imagination, sprung straight from the heart and free of any literary conventions, and work best when heard beside a winter fire crackling in the hearth, passed on through generations of retelling by wandering tale-spinners and old country women. I render them from memory with no attempt to make them literary because I know that when they are tampered with they lose all their magic.

W.S.K.

The Eye of the Sea

WHEN YOU GO into the region of Morskie Oko in the Carpathian Mountains, and when you climb the steep mountain road that leads to the strange black-water lake which nestles among the crags, you find a curious sadness in the hushed, stilled landscape, and this tale tells you why. In Polish, Morskie Oko means The Eye of the Sea, and how it got its name is part of this story.

A great Polish noble named Pan Morski lived there a long, long time ago, when there was nothing but rich fields of wheat, and rolling green pastures, and deep rustling woods where these huge mountains, cliffs and towering escarpments rise everywhere today. He was a rich and powerful landholder, fiercely devoted to his heritage, who took great pride in his family name that derives from the word for 'Sea,' but that's another story. The lands of a young and handsome Transylvanian prince began just beyond old Morski's property, a step or two from the heaped stone mounds with which the old warrior marked his boundary lines, so that the two nobles lived side-by-side like two country neighbors separated only by a strip of pasture. The old man didn't like the prince because he was a foreigner, but since they'd never done each other any harm they lived peaceably enough, and most people thought they'd live like that until the end of their appointed years.

But Morski had a daughter of such rare beauty that no one who saw her could believe his eyes. Everyone thought of this amazing beauty as a miracle, something that came directly from God, and many were struck with such awesome wonder that they lost their wits. It happened that the young prince caught sight of her one day, quite lost his mind over her, and did the one thing sure to drive the fierce old man into a towering rage: he asked for her in marriage. This so enraged old Morski that he swore he'd give his daughter to the Devil before a foreigner could have her. She was to marry one of her own kind, finding her husband among her own people, or no one at all.

Fate, however, is never to be challenged. The Devil's always listening,

11

ready to exploit every chance for mischief. Old Morski was a warrior. One day his king called him to a long campaign, and he went off to distant lands for many years to come, but first he locked his daughter behind convent walls, threatening to hurl a Father's Curse upon her if she married the handsome Transylvanian.

"May the Devil have you," he repeated, "if you disobey me!"

But he stayed away too long on the king's campaign, the young girl grew bored and restless in the nunnery and, in the meantime, the handsome Transylvanian continued his courtship. He sent her necklaces of such dazzling workmanship that they looked like the work of angels. He sent jewels and ribbons. He sent a troop of soothsayers, who were also sorcerers and witches, and who painted such a brilliant future for her with their glib Gypsy tongues that she was overwhelmed.

"You'll be a great lady," they told her, "with castles made of silver and rooms of pure gold."

They cast such a spell on the yearning and unhappy girl that she agreed to escape from the convent where her father placed her and to defy his wishes. At nightfall the prince himself came to the convent gate, dressed as a begging friar, and pleading for alms. He put on such a show of piety, and made so many signs of the cross, that the nuns took pity on him and let him inside. His soothsayers scattered magic herbs on the ground, and chanted strange words, and all the watchdogs fell asleep. The prince fled with the girl and immediately ordered that a palace made of coral be built for her at once, and then he had it studded with gold and priceless stones and jewels.

So the girl became a princess and danced all day among the flowers in the meadows, or played with her children, and in the evenings the prince's Gypsy women, witches and enchanters sang to her and told her the most amazing and wonderful stories so that she would have pleasant and lovely dreams. Everything there was like heaven. There was never hail falling from the sky to ruin the crops, nor any floods, nor did any sickness ever strike the cattle or the other livestock. In seven years she had seven children, and each grew tall and straight as a sapling and glowing with health.

In all that time Morski was far away, and no word of him came back to the country, so that people began to say that Tartars must have killed him. Since so many years had passed, the daughter believed this, dressed herself in mourning, claimed her father's lands, and thought she'd never have to worry about the curse with which he'd threatened her.

But one day he returned without a word of warning. "Where is my daughter?" he demanded, and people, always eager as they are for malicious mischief, quickly showed him the coral palace in which she was living.

She ran out to greet him, wearing her finest jewels, but the implacable old man hurled his curse upon her. He made the sign of the cross, spat three times on the ground, and stamped his foot so hard that the coral palace shattered and turned to dust.

"May your foreigner turn to stone!" he shouted. "And all his goods with him!"

The princess begged his forgiveness on her knees, and brought out all her children to move him to compassion, but the sight of them only enraged him more.

"May you melt in your own tears!" he cursed her. "And let your damned children drown in them as well, because you are no longer Morski's daughter and they are not his kind!"

A Father's Curse had its effect quickly in those days and Morski's came true at once. The fields, the meadows, the palaces, and the great herds of cattle and horses, turned immediately into one huge boulder. The prince went mad with terror and tried to escape disguised as a monk, but the curse reached him anyway and turned him into granite, and you can still see him there as that grey stone pillar that's known in the region as The Monk, and that stands above the lake today.

The Princess wept and pleaded and called on all her husband's witches to help her but they could do nothing against a Father's Curse. Each of them seized a child and began to run, but the ground burst apart under their feet, and huge mountains leaped up at every step they took, so they could not run far. Worn out, they all sat down. Death appeared before them. The frightened children cried out for their mother who came running to them but not all her tears could turn the curse away. She wept until great pools of tears formed everywhere around her and people even say that she wept out her eyes. One of them became the lake known as Morskie Oko, the Eye of the Sea, because that used to be her maiden name as well. The princess threw all her precious stones and jewels into that great pond but there is no use looking for them there because they've all been fished out many years ago.

Then, when there was nothing left around her except the lake, the gaunt grim cliffs and the seven pools of tears, the princess herself dissolved into the lake, and since she was still dressed in mourning for her father the water in the lake turned as black as her mourning robes, as you can see for yourself whenever you go there, while each of her seven children lies at the bottom of the seven pools.

People say that sobs and sighs can still be heard coming from that black water on a misty day, because a Father's Curse dooms a disobedient child to endless suffering, and peace can never come to the princess' soul. But if you're moved to pity when you hear this story, or if you mourn for her when you hear her weeping, be sure you make a sign of the cross, spit and stamp your foot three times on the ground, or you'll be buried under an avalanche of snow falling off the mountains.

Seized by the Wind

EVERYONE KNOWS that there are sorcerers and witches who can do a lot of harm if they get annoyed, and there was once a powerful and evil sorcerer who got angry at a young, decent peasant lad. No one remembers now what made him so angry but he decided on a terrible revenge none the less.

One day, while the lad was working in his master's fields, the sorcerer slipped into his cottage and stuck a new, freshly sharpened knife under the threshold. Then he muttered a curse that summoned all the winds and told them to seize the poor lad, carry him away, and keep him whirling in the sky for seven long years.

The lad went out the next day to stack hay in the meadow when suddenly a great whirlwind came out of nowhere, scattered the haystacks all over the province, and snatched up the lad. The brave young man struggled as best he could. He clutched at fenceposts and grasped at tree branches with his strong, young hands, but it was all in vain. A powerful force swept him on and carried him off no matter what he did. He flew on and on like a wild pigeon, just over the rooftops and with the good, firm earth just beyond his reach. The sun was already setting in the west, and the hungry lad looked down with longing at the smoking chimneys in the villages that he could almost brush with his feet in passing, but all his shouts, cries, and pleas for help went unheard in the howling gale.

The winds carried him like that for three months or more without food or water and the poor lad dried out like a pine board in the sun but there was nothing he could do about it. The sorcerer's curse was so powerful that not even prayers helped. Besides, the roaring of the wind drowned out all his prayers. He flew to many places, seeing many things, but most of the time the wind kept him whirling in the sky just over his village.

Lost, hungry, thirsty and alone, he looked through his tears at his master's cottage. He saw his master's daughter who loved him and whom he hoped to marry. It was close to noon and she was carrying dinner in a basket to her

15

father's laborers in the fields, but no matter how he tried he couldn't reach out far enough to touch her. He tried to call her name but his weak voice died in his dried-out throat so that he sounded like just another blackbird, and she didn't even look up to see him right above her head.

Then, down below, he saw the evil sorcerer who looked up and shouted: "You'll fly like this for seven years, with neither food nor drink, but you'll stay alive. And you'll be whirling up there, just above your village, so you'll be able to see everything you're missing and suffer all the more."

Then the sorcerer turned into an eagle and flew up to circle over the lad and amuse himself with his misery and sadness.

"Please, Father Eagle," begged the lad. "Forgive me for whatever I've done to make you so angry. Look at me! My lips have cracked. My throat is as dry as an empty bucket. My hands and my face are all bone, with no flesh anywhere on me. Let me go! Take pity on my suffering!"

The sorcerer muttered a short incantation and the lad at once stopped whirling in the air and hung suspended in one place although his feet still couldn't touch the ground.

"It's a good thing you're apologizing," he said to the lad, "but it's not enough. What else will you promise me if I let you go?"

"Anything!" cried the lad, folded his hands as if for prayer, and knelt in the air. "Take anything you want?"

"Anything? Well, in that case I'll take the one thing that really matters to you," said the sorcerer. "I'll take your girl and marry her myself. So if you'll give her up, here and now, I'll let you walk on the ground once more."

This was a terrible decision for the lad to make but he had no choice. Besides, he reasoned that he'd find some way to save the girl, and himself as well, once he was back on earth, while up in the sky he'd always be helpless.

"Alright," he said sadly. "You demand a terrible sacrifice from me. But since there's no other way, let it be as you want."

The sorcerer breathed on him and the lad stood firmly on the ground again. He fell to his knees and he kissed the earth, happy to be out of the clutches of the wind, and then he jumped up and ran as fast as he could to his master's cottage. He met his girl in the door as she was going out for the evening milking, and she cried out, amazed to see this dried-out, bony apparition, and burst into tears, because she loved him and thought he had disappeared for good, and she'd wept long and hard over him the three months he was gone.

He wanted to kiss and comfort her, but he was bound by his promise to the sorcerer, so he pushed her away with his skeletal hands and arms, and went in to see her father for whom he'd worked so loyally for so many years, and who had always treated him well and fairly, almost like a son.

"Father!" he cried. "I won't work for you any more. Nor can I marry your daughter. I love her dearer than my own two eyes but she can't be mine."

The grey-haired old master looked at him, surprised, and asked what had happened. Then, noticing the suffering stamped into the lad's face, which had once been ruddy and full of health but was now gaunt and pale, he understood that there was witchcraft involved in this matter and let the boy tell his tale in his own good time.

The wretched lad told him everything that happened. He told about the whirlwind, and his flight over the rooftops, and the promise he'd been forced to give to the sorcerer.

"I've got to do something about this," said the desperate young man, "but I don't know how."

The master listened patiently until he'd heard it all and told the boy to cheer up.

"Things are never so bad that there isn't a good way out of it," he said. "And if an evil sorcerer casts a spell on you, there are good witches to turn the tables on him."

He got up, picked up a hefty purse, and went to see a witch who lived in the forest just beyond the village. He was back for supper, as pleased as if he was already holding his daughter's children on his knees, and said to the lad: "Go see the witch at daybreak tomorrow and all will be well."

The tired lad collapsed into a deep sleep but he awoke well before the sunrise and went to the witch as he had been told. He found her in her house, by her fireplace, as she was burning magic herbs to make a good spell.

"Stand still," she ordered him. "Don't move until I tell you. And don't be frightened by what you see and hear."

Then she threw more herbs into the fire, cried a magic word, and at once a terrible wind returned and swept above the forest. The lad stood still. He hardly dared to breathe until the witch took him by the arm and led him into her yard outside.

"Look up," she told him.

The lad looked up and was amazed to see the evil sorcerer high up in the air, turning cartwheels with only his nightshirt on.

"There's your enemy," said the witch. "But he can't harm you now. If you want him to watch your wedding, which will hurt him more than anything I can do, do what I will teach you and he'll get a good taste of the suffering he imposed on a decent lad."

The delighted lad ran home and a month later he and his girl were married. His old master, now his father-in-law, gave them a sumptuous wedding. But while all the guests were dancing in the house, the young man stepped out into the yard. He looked up and saw the sorcerer again, still in his flying nightshirt, doing his cartwheels endlessly just above the house.

"You should come closer for a better look," the happy bridegroom said, "but after that I don't want to see you anywhere again."

Then he did exactly as the witch had taught him, took a new, freshly-sharpened knife out of his boot, threw it at the sorcerer, and hit him in the leg. The sorcerer fell to earth but the knife pinned him firmly to the ground right outside the window, and there he stood the whole night through, looking at the good times of the wedding party and the dancing guests.

The next day he was gone and no one in the village ever saw him again. But other people saw him as he flew over a distant village, and then across a lake two more miles away. He rode a whirlwind, with a great flock of ravens and magpies in front and behind him, whose shrill screams and cawing announced his coming until the end of time.

The Glass Mountain

THERE WAS ONCE a high mountain, made of purest glass, that nobody could climb because its steep sides were as hard and smooth as only glass could make them, and there was neither a handhold nor a foothold anywhere on it.

No one had ever been to the top of the mountain but everybody knew that an enchanted castle, made wholly out of gold, stood there among the clouds, and that a tree that bore golden apples grew in front of it. An enchanted princess more beautiful than all the treasures of the world slept in a silver room in that golden castle. She had been put there by a jealous witch who envied her beauty, and she was doomed to stay there, asleep and waiting in her silver room behind the golden walls, until some brave young man found a way to climb the glass mountain and pick a golden apple off the magic tree.

The witch made sure that everybody knew about the princess in the golden castle, about her countless treasures, her cellars filled throughout with precious stones and jewels, and about the chambers full of chests of gold, so that many brave young men would attempt to scale the glass mountain and waken the princess. The bravest and the hardiest knights had come for years to the foot of the enchanted mountain but none could reach the top.

Seven years passed as the princess waited for her rescuer, watching brave knights who tried one by one to scale the glass mountain, only to slip, slide down the precipice, and twist their necks at the bottom of the slope. Some managed to reach halfway to the top, with the sharp iron shoes of their horses helping to take them there, but sooner or later all of them fell and tumbled back and broke their arms and legs and their heads as well. The beautiful princess looked sadly from her window at the handsome knights as they struggled upward, and then at the many others, along with their horses, who lay dead or dying at the foot of the cruel mountain.

She longed for rescue and she also wished that the handsome knights wouldn't keep on dying, but they kept coming from all over the world, because they had all heard about her beauty and the treasures of the golden castle.

Three days were left of the seventh year when a knight in a golden armor came to the bottom of the glassy slope. Many other knights were assembled there but he ordered them to stand aside and charged the glass mountain. He reached halfway to the top, as high as any other knight had ever come before, and then he rode back down without a mishap as all the others watched in surprise and awe.

Next day at dawn he tried it again, set his horse to the gallop and charged up the slope as though it were a flat and level plain. Sparks flew from under his horse's hooves as he passed the halfway mark but he kept on coming. The knights below were watching in amazement as he went up and up until, at last, he stood under the branches of the apple tree. But then a great black hawk swooped out of the branches. Its wings hissed through the air and its talons slashed. It struck the horse right between the eyes. The poor, shocked beast reared on its hind legs, its nostrils distended and eyes wild with terror. It snorted, neighed, and its mane rose wildly, and then its hooves slipped over the edge of the mountain. It toppled backwards together with its rider, and they gouged a deep furrow in the smooth glass slope as they slid headlong to the bottom. Nothing was left of the brave knight and his gallant charger except broken bones that rattled in the crushed and dented armor like peas in a tin cup or a leather bag.

One day was left to the end of the seventh year when a poor but handsome young scholar appeared. He was tall and strong even though he was barely out of boyhood and he was determined to succeed where the others failed. He stood and watched quietly while the knights charged the slope on horseback and broke their necks for nothing and then he started to climb it slowly and patiently on foot. While still at home, he had been thinking for more than a year about the enchanted princess in her golden castle, held as the spellbound prisoner of an evil witch on top of a glass mountain, and he decided on a way to free her. He went to a nearby forest, trapped and killed a wildcat, and fastened its long, sharp claws to his own hands and feet. Equipped with such climbing tools, he clawed his way boldly halfway up the mountain and then he had to rest.

THE GLASS MOUNTAIN

He was so weary that he could hardly breathe. The sun was setting and he hadn't eaten anything all day. Thirst tortured him. He begged a passing cloud for a single raindrop to moisten his mouth but the cloud floated quietly by and gave him no help.

His feet were cut and bleeding and he could hold onto the cold, glassy slope only with his hands.

He knew that the golden apples were guarded by the black falcon that had destroyed the knight in the golden armor. Some people even said that the deadly bird was really the disguised evil witch who flew at night around the top of the mountain like a sentinel, and here night was coming because the sun was down on the horizon. When the brave lad looked up he had to tilt his head so far back to see the distant summit that his warm sheepskin cap fell off and he was left bareheaded in the wind. When he looked down he saw the precipice below. He knew that death was waiting for him there, as she had waited for all the others like him who had tried to conquer the terrible glass mountain. He also knew that from this point on, the slopes went straight up, as smooth and vertical as a the neck of a bottle or a marble pillar.

Then, suddenly, the sun was gone. Everything was dark. The stars threw only a dim light on the slope ahead, and the young climber clung with bleeding hands to the sheer glass mountain as if he were bolted into it. He was too tired to go on. He could go neither up nor down anyway now that night had come and he knew that his strength wouldn't last much longer. He thought again about the beautiful princess who was waiting for him in her silver room, and about the golden apples and the golden castle and the chambers full of gold and precious stones. He knew then that he would never see his home again and waited for death to come and carry him away.

Tired as he was, he quite forgot where he was and nodded off to sleep. But even though he slept until almost midnight, he had dug his sharp wildcat claws into the glass so deeply that they kept him hanging on the mountain wall like a painting, or a tapestry, or a holy icon.

The midnight moon had barely risen from behind a cloud when the great black hawk shot upward from its apple tree and started circling the top of the mountain. Hungry and looking for fresh carrion it could eat, it saw the sleeping lad and swooped down upon him. But the brave youth was no longer sleeping; he had seen the hawk and now thought of a way to use him to get off the mountain.

He waited until the huge bird dug its long, sharp talons deep into his body, withstood the pain bravely, and suddenly reached up and caught the hawk by its two scaly feet. Startled, the bird shot straight into the air, and carried the young scholar high over the castle, where they flew round and round a tall golden tower that shined like a lamp in the silver moonlight.

The brave lad hung on no matter how hard the hawk tried to shake him off. He looked down at the gleaming castle that seemed as if it was made out of golden fires. He saw the tall windows of the purest crystal glittering with jewels. He saw the beautiful spellbound princess sitting on her balcony, sunk deep in her thoughts and pondering her sad fate. Then, seeing that the hawk had brought him close to the apple tree, he pulled his penknife from inside his belt — the same sharp knife he used for trimming writing quills in school — and slashed off both of the great bird's feet, along with the talons sunk into his own back.

The hawk screamed in pain, beat its huge black wings and vanished inside a cloud, and the brave, clever and determined lad tumbled down into the branches of the apple tree, among the golden apples.

Once in the tree, the tired youth pried the hawk's talons from his flesh and threw them away. A touch with a golden apple healed all his wounds at once. A dragon breathed fire on him at the castle gate and tried to bar his way, but the lad threw a golden apple at the beast and it leaped into the moat, vanished and was never seen again.

Then the golden gates of the castle fell open before him with a crash and the brave young man saw a courtyard filled with rare trees and flowers, and high up on her tower balcony sat the enchanted princess with all of her ladies. Seeing her rescuer, she ran down to greet him as her lord and husband, gave him all her treasures, and that's how the poor young scholar became a great lord. But he never returned to earth again because only the witch herself, disguised as the black hawk, could have brought him and his beautiful wife back to the good, firm soil of the plains below, and only she could have carried down the castle and all of its treasures. The black hawk, however, was never seen alive again. It died soon after it had lost its feet and was found some time later in a forest not far from the glass mountain.

It happened, though, that the rich young lord was walking through his gardens one day with his princess-wife, and looked down to see a vast crowd gathered at the foot of the sheer glass slope. He whistled up a swallow on his silver flute and sent it down to see what was happening down below the mountain.

The swallow soon returned, because it was spring, and said that everyone below was alive and happy because the death of the evil witch had ended all her spells.

"The hawk's blood," said the swallow, "has brought all the dead knights back to life. All those who died trying to scale the glass mountain woke up and rose today as if from a dream. They're mounting their horses, fresh as if born anew, and all the people far and wide are full of joy and wonder."

The Willow Flute

THERE WERE ONCE three sisters living in a village. Each was tall and pretty, with bright blue eyes and hair as fine as cornsilk, and each had many suitors who wanted to marry her. But the youngest was so beautiful that she made the others seem as bland and pale as candles beside the moon, so many young men who first fell in love with the oldest sister, or with the middle sister, soon forgot about them when they saw the youngest. The three sisters loved each other so they didn't mind, knowing they had lots of time in which to get married, but the oldest became envious and annoyed as the years went by and all her suitors ran after her youngest sister one after another. She resolved that the next time that happened she would have revenge.

All might have gone well, however, for many more years, if she didn't fall in love herself. One day a rich young lord came riding by as the three sisters were picking herbs and flowers for a wreath. The oldest sister gave him a long look, and loved him at once, but he fell in love with the youngest sister and asked for her hand.

A few days later the sisters went to pick berries in the forest and the oldest killed the youngest and buried her in a deep hole among the willows. The middle sister tried to protect the poor girl but failed to save her, and she said nothing when the two older sisters came home that night without her. The crime was so terrible, even in those times, that word of it couldn't pass her lips.

The oldest sister told their parents that wolves had carried off the youngest and no one had a reason to question her story. The young lord mourned the dead girl for a year but time soothed his grief. The murderess went out of her way to console him, seeming both kind and gentle and just as sad as he, and she got enough of a hold on his heart so that a few months later he asked for her hand and the day of the wedding was set.

Meanwhile, a willow tree had taken root on the grave of the murdered

25

sister. A young shepherd rested there one day while his flock grazed among the willows. He wanted to carve himself a reed pipe so he could play a tune, and cut a fresh young branch of the new-grown willow, and took it with him when he left to work on it at home.

He made a beautiful flute from the hollowed branch of the willow that grew on the grave of the murdered sister but no matter what tune he wished to play all he could hear was the same sad song piped in a plaintive voice.

> *"Play, shepherd, play, poor dear,*
> *May God spare you fear!*
> *My oldest sister dug this grave for me,*
> *My middle sister did her best for me.*
> *Play, shepherd, play my song*
> *To right a great wrong."*

Startled, the shepherd took his flute to the parents of the murdered girl, but no matter who tried to play a tune on it the sad song of the youngest sister came out the same way, changed only a little to fit the musician.

The mother was the first to try, and this is what she heard:

> *"Play, mother, play, my dear,*
> *May God dry your tears,*
> *Your oldest daughter dug a grave for me,*
> *Your middle daughter did her best for me.*
> *Play, mother, play my song*
> *To right a great wrong."*

Then the father took the flute into his hands and this is what he heard:

> *"Play, father, play, stop weeping,*
> *Stay in God's hands and keeping,*
> *Your oldest daughter put an end to me,*
> *Your middle daughter defended me.*
> *Play, father, play my song*
> *To right a great wrong."*

The middle sister burst into tears as she took the flute from her father's hands and this is what she heard:

> *"Play, sister, save your tears!*
> *God give you happy years!*
> *Our oldest sister will pay for her crime,*
> *But you'll be happy for the rest of time.*
> *Play, sister, play my song*
> *To right a great wrong."*

Hearing these songs, the murderess turned as pale a winding sheet, but she could not refuse to take the flute when her parents handed it to her. She no sooner touched it to her lips when the blood of the murdered sister flooded her face with guilt, and the willow flute sang for the last time.

"Play, sister, play!
God will make you pay!
Your envy killed me, not your knife,
Though Middle Sister tried to save my life.
Play, sister, play my song
To right your great wrong.

"Play, sister, play my ditty.
You showed me no pity!
A dark, deep grave is now my home,
I lie beneath the thick, black loam.
The willow sings my song
To right the great wrong."

Then everyone recognized the oldest sister for what she really was and what she had done. An innocent victim can cry out for justice even from the grave, and in those days everyone could hear much more than we do today.

The cruel oldest sister was punished at once. She was tied by her hands and feet to the tails of wild horses which tore her apart. And the young lord, feeling no longer any love or pity for the murderess, soon turned for consolation to the middle sister.

The Poor Countryman and the Greedy Hag

THERE WAS ONCE a poor old man living in a forest, who made a skimpy livelihood by collecting twigs that he sold for kindling, and although he'd worked hard all his life he had nothing to show for it in the end. But one day, as he was cutting down a tree, he heard a cry for help and saw a man, his wagon and his horses sinking in a quagmire. He ran at once to help, pulled them all to safety on firm soil, and the rescued man told him that he could have anything he wanted.

"I am a great magician," the man said. "Whatever you want is yours for the asking."

The poor countryman had never had anything of value, so he didn't know what to ask for now that his chance had come, but while he stood there and scratched his head, wondering what to say, the magician gave him a big ram with a golden fleece.

"Whenever you shake this ram," he told the countryman, "gold ducats will fall out of his fleece."

The countryman said his thanks, took the ram to his poor hut in the forest and gave him a good shake, and at once gold coins spilled out of the ram's fleece.

His happiness, however, didn't last a month. Good fortune causes gossip, and gossip finds sharp ears, and it wasn't long before the story got to a certain old hag, said to be a witch, who lived near the forest. She made the countryman drunk one day, stole the magic ram, and put another in his place. The next day, needing another ducat, the countryman shook his ram again but no gold came flying from his fleece. The ram bleated and struggled to get away but not a penny appeared anywhere near him.

The poor old man went sadly to the quagmire, where he thought he might as well put an end to his life and be done with it, but the magician was waiting for him there and gave him a hen.

29

"Every time you want a golden egg," he said, "just ask this hen and she will lay it for you."

The countryman took the hen home but the old hag soon found out about her and made him drunk again. She stole the magic hen and put another in her place, and no matter how the poor old man asked this new hen for a golden egg she would never lay one. The witch got whatever golden eggs there were.

Sad once again, the poor countryman complained to the magician who gave him a magic tablecloth which spread itself with all and any food and drink that anyone might want.

"All that you have to do is say 'Tablecloth, tablecloth, spread thyself,'" the magician said, "and you will always have enough to eat."

Curious, the old man ordered the tablecloth to spread itself right there in the forest, and ate and drank so much that he fell asleep. But the hag was watching from behind a tree, and stole the tablecloth and slipped him another.

This time, however, the simple old man wasn't fooled so easily. He caught onto the old witch's tricks, went to the magician and asked him for something that would give the thieving hag a beating, and help him get back his ram, his hen and his tablecloth.

"Alright, but this is the last thing I can do for you," the magician said and gave him a wicker basket with two thick cudgels lying on the bottom. "All that you have to do is cry out 'Fiddlesticks, fiddlesticks come out of the basket,' and these two cudgels will jump right out of it and beat whoever you point to for as long as you want."

The countryman was delighted, thanked the kind magician and promised never to bother him again. Then he ran with his basket to the witch's house and knocked on her door.

"Who's there?" she shouted. "And what do you want?"

"It's me," the countryman said. "I've a magic basket that I want to show you."

She let him in at once and offered him a drink to put him to sleep, but he only shouted: "Fiddlesticks, fiddlesticks, come out of the basket," and pointed to the witch, and the two thick cudgels leaped out and started thrashing the hag without mercy.

She promised to give him back everything she'd stolen and begged his forgiveness, but the countryman let the cudgels go on with their work. She brought back the ram and the hen and the tablecloth, and all the golden coins and eggs that she had collected, but the countryman told the cudgels to keep pounding on her, because she was an evil old woman who had done a great deal of harm to many other people.

Then, finally, when she gave up the ghost, he said to his cudgels: "Fiddlesticks, fiddlesticks, back into my basket," and they jumped in at once.

Then, having a ram that spilled golden coins from his fleece each time he was shaken, a hen that laid a golden egg each time she was asked, a tablecloth that spread itself with a royal banquet any time he wished, and a pair of stout cudgels to thrash anyone who got in his way, he left the forest, went out into the world and joined the court of a certain king where he became a great and powerful lord.

Later, when the king had a war, the clever countryman defeated all his enemies, married the king's daughter, and became the ruler of the entire country when the old king died.

Pan Twardowski

THERE WAS ONCE a nobleman named Twardowski who lived near Krakow and didn't feel like dying. He was a wellborn member of the landed gentry on both his father's and his mother's side, and he lacked for nothing, but he had the itch to know more than good people should and he decided to find a cure for death.

One day he read in an old book how to summon the Devil, so he crept quietly out of the city just before midnight, came to Podgorze at the foot of the mountains, and started calling out in a loud, deep voice. The Devil came at once, quick as lightning and as smooth as butter, and they made a deal in just the way that such things were done in those times. The Devil immediately scribbled out a contract, using his own knee for a writing-table, and Twardowski signed in blood drawn from his ring finger.

Among the many clauses was this main condition: that the Devil would have no claims on Twardowski's soul, or access to his body, until he caught him visiting in Rome. Since Twardowski had no intention of traveling abroad he thought he was safe. Having indentured the Devil as his servant, he ordered him to bring him all the silver to be found in Poland, bury it in one place and cover it well with sand. He pointed to the town of Olkusz as he gave these orders; the obedient Devil brought the silver there; and that's how the famous silver mines of Olkusz got their start.

Then he demanded, on a whim, that the Devil bring a huge rock or boulder to the top of a cliff called Pieskowa Skala, balance it on its point and make it stand there for all time. The eager servant did as his master ordered, and the tall stone stands there to this day, balanced on its narrow end on top of the mountain.

After that Twardowski could have anything he wanted. He became a famous sorcerer and healer, curing diseases that no other doctor could do anything about. He would ride painted horses, right out of a canvas, and flew through the air without any wings. If he felt like taking a long trip somewhere he'd mount a rooster with a fiery tail and travel faster than any horse could run. The Devil gave him knowledge that no decent people ought to have. He went sailing with his lover on the Vistula, riding a boat that had neither sails nor oars, and he made it run upriver against the current. What's more, he could set fire to a village a hundred leagues away with just a piece of glass clutched in his right hand.

One day he saw a girl he thought he'd like to marry but this didn't prove as easy as all that. She was the daughter of a wealthy potter, who confounded many other suitors with a curious riddle, and she prepared to test Twardowski as well. She hid an insect in a small stone flask and said she'd marry only the man who guessed what it was.

"What is this creature?" she asked. "An insect or snake? You'll be my man if you make no mistake."

Twardowski, who had come calling on her disguised as a beggar, saw right through the stone flask and saw a small bee.

"I see a small bee," he said, "as sure as my life, so I'm now your man and you are my wife."

Caught in her own trap, the girl had to marry the supposed beggar and Twardowski never told her who he really was. She built a small clay hut in the market square in Krakow, where she sold pots and bowls that Twardowski would order his servants to smash each time he and his retainers rode by in his splendid coach.

Gold was like sand to him because the Devil brought him mountains of it every time he wanted. One day, after amusing himself with black magic until he got tired, he went for a stroll in a deep, dark forest and there the Devil jumped on him and told him it was time for him to go to Rome. The sorcerer lost his temper, hurled a secret word at the Devil and drove him away. Enraged, the Devil pulled up a pine tree by the roots and hit Twardowski so hard with it that he lamed one of his legs, so that from then on the necromancer was known in Krakow as Limpy.

Things went like that for years and the Devil got tired of waiting for Twardowski's soul. He came to the sorcerer disguised as a courtier and said that his master, a rich foreign lord, was ill in a tavern and needed a healer. Twardowski followed this supposed courtier to a nearby inn, not knowing that the name of the inn was Rome, but he had no sooner stepped across the threshold when a vast swarm of ravens, owls and screechowls settled on the roof, croaking and screeching until the rafters rang. Twardowski guessed at once what might happen to him so he snatched a newborn infant from its cradle and clutched it to his chest. He stood there, shaking like a leaf in terror, while the Devil leaped into the room in his normal form. Though he was handsomely dressed in a tricorn hat, a German frock-coat with a long vest that covered his belly, tight pantaloons, silk stockings with ribbons for garters and shoes with silver buckles, everyone knew at once who he was because his horns stuck out from under his hat, his claws protruded through the toes of his shoes, and the cue of his powdered wig curled up like a tail from the back of his head.

He reached for Twardowski, ready to carry him away, but then he saw the innocent, newly-christened infant to which he had no right.

"Put it down," he said.

"I won't," said Twardowski.

"What?" said the Devil. "Aren't you a noble? *'Verbum nobile debet esse stabile,'* he quoted in Latin. "A noble's word must always be kept. You gave your word that you'd be mine in Rome, and this inn is called Rome, isn't it? So do what you promised."

Twardowski knew that he couldn't break his word as a gentleman and that the game was up. He put the infant back in its cradle and, immediately, he and the Devil flew out through the chimney.

The crows, ravens, owls and other night birds screamed out in delight and all of them swept up into the sky together, but Twardowski didn't lose heart no matter how high they flew. He looked down, saw the good earth so far below that villages were like gnats, great cities looked like flies on a wall, and Krakow itself seemed no bigger than two spiders together. Sorrow squeezed his heart at the thought that he was leaving everything he loved and all the people he had learned to care for. Then, flying so high among the winds that neither the vultures nor the Carpathian eagles could reach him, he found the strength to hum a holy anthem.

It was one of those canticles in honor of the Holy Mother that he had composed while he was still a youth, when his soul was pure, and he knew nothing of sorcery, book-learning or magic.

Though he sang with all his heart and soul, the winds seized his voice and carried it away. His hymn didn't rise with him towards the heavens but fell back to earth so that it might uplift the souls of good, simple people, and the shepherds heard him as they lay with their flocks on the mountainsides below, and their hearts lifted towards God and goodness.

Twardowski sang and sang, carried ever higher, so that all the people heard him everywhere on earth, and then his voice gave out and he could sing no more. But then he saw that he was motionless, suspended in the air, and that the Devil had vanished and left him alone, and then he heard a great voice thundering in the clouds.

"It's never too late to mend your ways," the great voice told him, "but I can't let you back on earth among decent people until you've paid for dealing with the Devil, so you'll stay up here until Judgment Day."

His song is silent now. His voice is no longer heard anywhere on earth. But old men who remember ancient times used to point until quite recent days to the dark spot on the crescent moon where Pan Twardowski sits and waits for the final judgment and the end of the world.

The Wild Geese

IT'S SAID that in the old days, when parents cast a curse on their children or other relations, their words would come true at once.

A certain wellborn girl had a lover whom her mother refused to accept as her future husband. But since the girl loved him more each day, and didn't want to break her engagement to him, the mother threatened her with a curse.

"I'd rather see our whole family turn into wild geese," she said angrily. "Than that your lover should become your husband!"

She had no sooner spoken than that wish came true. The father, mother, sisters and brothers turned into birds and flew off at once to join a flock of wild geese on a nearby lake, and so did the young girl and her unlucky lover. The two lovers stayed together through summer and winter on another pond.

But a hunter saw them there one day, thought that he'd like roast goose for his dinner, shot at one and brought down the goose that had been the girl. She fell out of the air into a tuft of swamp-grass where the reeds held her as if in a cage. The hunter rowed out to her and found that she had not been hit. She had been merely deafened by his gun. He took her home and put her behind the stove to fatten her up, thinking that Christmas would be the time to eat her. But because he was unmarried and didn't have much money he had to keep house for himself, and as often happens in a home which doesn't have a woman to keep things in order, the whole place needed sweeping, cleaning, polishing and attention.

Next morning he went out early, locking the door carefully behind him, because he didn't want anyone to come in and see the way he was living. But when he came back he was amazed to see that, while he was gone, someone had cleaned and straightened his entire house. The bed was made, the floor had been scrubbed, the walls were swept clean of cobwebs, the pots and pans had all been washed and polished, and his dinner was cooked and waiting for him on the table.

Puzzled, he decided to hide in the attic the next day to see who'd come in and how they would do it with the door locked against them. He drilled a hole in the attic floor, so that he could peer down into the room below, and saw the goose skip from behind the stove, shake off her feathers and turn into a wonderfully beautiful young girl, who immediately set about cleaning his house and cooking his dinner.

Unable to believe his eyes, he pretended to go out the next day as well, but only hid behind the door and waited. Then, as soon as the goose shook off her feathers, turned into the girl and started making up his bed, he leaped inside and seized her in his arms. She struggled and protested and tried to turn back into a goose again but he swept up all her feathers and locked them in a cupboard. He thought that if he burned them straight away she'd never be able to fly away from him, but since he needed new feathers for a featherbed he saved them instead.

In time the hunter married the young girl. She made a good wife and she made him happy and he forgot about the feathers locked up in the cupboard. Then, one day, in that time of year when wild geese fly to warmer lands, he fell asleep with his head in her lap as she sat on the doorstep dreaming of her lover.

Two wild geese flew by, calling out to her, and she knew that they were both her sisters. "Our little sister sits home with her husband," they called down from the sky. "Come with us, little one!"

"God be with you forever," she called out to them. "I can't fly with you ever!"

Two more geese flew by, and these were her brothers, and they too called her to come flying with them, but she said the same thing to them as to her two sisters. "God be with you forever, I can't fly with you ever!"

Then two more wild geese passed overhead, and these were her parents, and they also called: "Our little daughter sits home with her husband. Fly with us, little one!"

And she said again: "God be with you forever, I can't fly with you ever."

Then a solitary wild goose flew by all alone, and this was her lover from the nearby pond, and he called out sadly: "My love sits home with the hunter. Fly with me, my love!"

At this she lifted her husband's head gently off her lap so as not to wake him, and went to the cupboard and dressed in her feathers, and then she flew straight out of the window to be with her lover. None of this would have happened if the hunter had used his head when he had the chance, and burned all her feathers, but when a man takes his wife for granted he's likely to lose her.

About Two Babies Cast Onto the Waters

A LONG TIME AGO, longer than most people can remember, there were three young and pretty sisters living in a poor hut in a little village. One evening, with nothing but a crust of bread to eat for their supper, they talked about the kind of men each of them wished to marry.

"I want a baker for a husband," said the oldest sister, "because I'd always have freshbaked buns to eat."

"I want a cook," said the middle sister, "because I love good soup."

"The only man I want to marry is our own prince," said the youngest sister, "because I had a dream about the children we would have. If we had a son, pure gold would pour out of his bath instead of bathwater. And if we had a daughter, real roses would bloom in her cheeks whenever she smiled, and real pearls would fall from her eyes whenever she cried."

The prince, who had a habit of walking near the poor cottages in the evenings, so that he might hear what his subjects wanted and what they thought of him, stood just outside their window as the sisters talked. Next day he summoned them to appear before him and asked each what she wished for the night before.

"I wished to marry the royal baker," said the oldest, and the prince said that she would have her wish.

"I wished to marry the royal cook," said the middle sister, and the prince also granted her the husband she wanted.

But when he asked the youngest girl what she had wished the most she was afraid to say it, and hesitated to tell him about her dream, so he encouraged her with every kindness until she knelt before him and confessed the kind of husband she wanted to marry.

He raised her up then, seated her on the throne beside him, and said: "Your wish is fulfilled."

Three great weddings took place shortly afterwards. But the two older sisters were jealous of the young princess' happiness, which came to her so

41

unexpectedly, and secretly connived against her. The prince was away when the youngest sister gave birth to a boy, and they stole the baby, replaced it with a puppy, and sent word to the absent prince that instead of a son whose bathwater turned to liquid gold, his wife had given birth to a mongrel dog. The same thing happened later when the princess had a little daughter, only this time the sisters said it was a kitten. In each case they took the newborn baby, put it in a box, and sent it down a river that flowed near the castle.

The prince, who was away at a distant war, and had many dangerous matters on his mind, was quite enraged by these messages.

"You promised me a son whose bathwater turned to liquid gold," he wrote to his wife, "and you gave me a dog. And instead of a daughter who wept real pearls you've given me a kitten."

Then he ordered her walled up alive in the castle dungeons and the cruel sisters saw to it that the order was carried out at once.

But God takes note of everything that happens. An angel brought the princess food and drink in her cell whenever she felt either thirst or hunger. God also saw to it that the little children who had been cast adrift were found, each in his and her turn, by a kindly fisherman who plucked them out of the river, and took them both home to raise, having no other children of his own. He was, of course, surprised when pure gold flowed out of the basin whenever he bathed his adopted son, while real roses bloomed in his daughter's cheeks, and real pearls fell from her eyes whenever she wept. Thanks to this, the kindly fisherman came to a great fortune and built a golden house within its own forest, for the abandoned orphans.

It was there that one night the children had a dream. They both dreamed that somewhere nearby was a crystal spring whose waters shot one hundred yards straight into the air, and that this living water would create such springs wherever it was taken. They also dreamed of a singing tree and of a bird that talked.

The next day, therefore, the boy went bravely into the forest to look for those wonders. But along the way he met a silver-haired old man who asked where he was going.

"I'm looking for a spring whose waters shoot straight up into the air," said the boy, "and for a singing tree and a bird who talks."

"Yes, well, they're all over there together," the old man pointed deep into the forest. "But be careful, lad. You'll hear a terrible thundering behind you when you draw that water but if you look around you will turn to stone."

The boy thanked him, went on and found the magic spring, but he got frightened when he heard the thundering behind him, glanced back to see what it was, and turned at once into a roadside boulder. His sister missed him when he didn't come home after a while and went looking for him, and she took along a water jug, just in case he had found the mysterious spring.

But on her way she met the same old, silver-haired man who gave her the same warning as he gave her brother, but then he added that she should plug her ears when leaving the spring.

"And oh, yes, before I forget," he said. "Sprinkle the water from the jug to right and left as you walk away."

The girl did everything the old man had told her and, at once, she heard a tree singing right next to her, and then a small, brightly-colored bird flew in and called out a greeting. Moreover, her brother jumped out of a roadside boulder and came running to her, as alive and healthy as he had been before. They went home together, and both the singing tree and the talking bird followed close behind.

Meanwhile, the prince had truly suffered the loss of his wife. He loved her dearly and he could not forgive himself for his hasty order. Looking for distraction and for peace of mind, he ordered a great hunt in the forest where his children lived. The boy, curious about the call of the hunting horns and the barking of dogs, joined the royal hunters, and shot a hare with an ordinary bow in the presence of the prince himself. The prince awarded him the hare and told him to take it home for dinner.

"Moreover," he said, "I'll come and help you eat it."

As soon as the lad brought the hare to his sister, they started worrying what they should serve the prince when he came for dinner, but the talking bird offered a suggestion.

"Roast the hare on the branches of the tree that followed you here," he said to the girl. "Then cook some noodles garnished with your pearls. The spring water you've brought in the jug ought to do the rest."

The girl did just what the bird suggested, but the cunning creature had yet another service to perform. The prince admired the golden house and the dishes garnished with the pearls, and the bird piped up immediately:

"Why are you so astonished, highness? After all, these pearls come from your daughter's eyes, just as your wife foretold. And this house is poured of the gold that flowed instead of water from each of your son's baths."

When the prince realized whose children these were, he kissed them both and asked the bird if it could tell him anything about their mother.

"She's just fine," the bird said. "An angel has been taking care of all her needs. And since she was unfairly imprisoned, time was ordered to stand still for her until her release. She looks and feels just like she did when you saw her last."

The prince rushed to the dungeons, ordered the walls torn down, and when the princess emerged into the light she was as pink-cheeked and healthy as she was on her wedding day.

From that time on, all of them lived long and happily together, except the two evil and conniving sisters, whom the prince ordered put to death. They were ripped apart with iron harrows in an open field and everyone agreed that justice was done.

The Oak Plucker and the Mountain Toppler

IT HAPPENED MANY YEARS AGO that the wife of a hunter, who was gathering berries in a forest, gave birth to twin boys and died soon afterwards, so that there was no one to care for the infants. One was suckled by a she-wolf, the other by a she-bear and the two lads grew up strong and free among the animals. The one who was brought up by the wolves was named Mountain Toppler because he was so immensely powerful that he could topple mountains, while the one whom the bears adopted was called The Oak Plucker because he could rip the sturdiest oaks right out of the ground as if they were wheat stalks.

They loved each other like good brothers should and decided to see the world together so they left the forest and set out on a journey. The first two days went well for them because they were still walking along the forest track but on the third day they ran into trouble. A high, steep mountain barred their way and they had to stop.

"What shall we do now, brother?" Oak Plucker called out sadly. "Is our journey over?"

"Don't worry about it, brother," said the Mountain Toppler. "I'll just toss this mountain to the side and our road will be clear."

As good as his word, Mountain Toppler put his back against the mountain, heaved, and pushed it aside for half a mile, and the two brothers continued on their way.

Then a gigantic oak tree towered over them, blocking the path ahead, so Oak Plucker stepped up, threw his arms around the massive trunk, ripped the tree out of the ground along with all its roots and hurled it into a river that flowed nearby.

But, strong as they were, their legs got tired after a few days so they lay down to rest. Sleep hadn't quite sealed their eyes when they saw a small man running towards them at such speed that no bird or animal would be able to

45

catch up with him. Amazed, they both stood up while the little man darted up to them.

"How are you doing, lads?" he cried out cheerfully. "I see you're tired out. How would you like a ride on a magic carpet? I've got one right here and I'll take you anywhere you want."

With this he unrolled a beautiful carpet, sat down on it and beckoned to the brothers.

"Come on," he said. "Try it out and you'll know what it feels like to fly like a bird."

Oak Plucker and Mountain Toppler stretched out comfortably on the carpet beside the little man, he clapped his hands, and the carpet soared high into the air as if it had wings.

"Not bad, is it?" the little man piped up after a while. "It's a good way to travel. Would you like to know, by the way, how I can run so fast? I got a pair of carpet slippers from a sorcerer and when I put them on they work like this carpet. One step takes me a mile ahead, and a good leap will carry me two miles."

The brothers begged him at once to give them each a slipper because they had a long way to go and their legs tired faster than the rest of them, and the little man was moved by their pleading. He gave them each a slipper and put them back on the ground again near a vast, rich city where there was a dragon that devoured many people every day.

The king of this country had announced that he would give one of his two daughters to the man who managed to kill this monster, and that the man would also get his throne after the king's death.

Oak Plucker and Mountain Toppler went at once to the palace, asked to see the king, and announced that they were willing to tackle the dragon. They were shown the dark cave in which the dragon lived and they went there without another thought. But halfway to the entrance the little man appeared again before them.

"So here you are again, lads!" the little man greeted them with pleasure. "I know why you're here but take a bit of good advice because that dragon is no joke. Each of you had better put on one of your slippers because when that monster leaps out of his cave he won't give you time to even wave your hand."

The brothers did as the little man advised. Oak Plucker positioned himself in front of the cave, holding a huge oak tree over his head so as to finish off the dragon with a single stroke as soon as he appeared, while

Mountain Toppler went to the back slope of the mountain which contained the cavern and started shaking it as if it were a bundle of dry straw.

The dragon leaped out of the cave so suddenly that Oak Plucker forgot about the tree he held in both hands over his head, and almost got eaten. But, luckily, he was wearing one of the magic slippers and jumped two miles aside in time to save himself. The dragon, unable to reach him, jumped over the mountain to get at Mountain Toppler who picked up the mountain and threw it at the monster so that it pinned its tail to the ground. Then Mountain Toppler also took a leap with his magic slipper and landed near his brother.

"Let's try again, brother," he called out. "This time we'll go together. The dragon can't move with his tail caught under a mountain. You crack his head with your oak tree and I'll finish him off with another mountain."

They marched up boldly to the dragon. One carried a big granite mountain and the other shook a huge oak tree mightily in the air. The dragon howled and gnashed his teeth like a pack of wolves when he saw his tormentors coming up again, and he wanted to throw himself at them and swallow them at one gulp as he'd done to others, but his tail was pinned firmly to the ground and he couldn't move. Oak Plucker spat in his hands, swung his tree and cracked the dragon's head so hard that splinters flew for miles, and Mountain Toppler hurled his mountain and buried the whole carcass.

Then the two brothers went back to the king who was waiting for them, and gave them each a beautiful princess for a bride, and when he died not long afterwards Oak Plucker and Mountain Toppler divided his kingdom, and lived in peace and plenty for the rest of their lives.

The Miller's Son

A CERTAIN MILLER had three sons. Two were smart and shrewd and the third was good-natured and a little stupid, and his two older brothers made him the butt of jokes as if he was a toy made for their amusement.

One day they said to him: "We're going to steal a pig from the rectory, just for a little fun. Meanwhile, you go to the charnel house and throw out all the bones."

The friendly dimwit spent the whole night doing what he was told to do, while his brothers sat at home laughing at the joke they had played on him.

But in the morning, back in the church and churchyard, the sexton came to ring the bells and heard something rattling in the charnel house. Seeing that bones were also flying out of there, he suspected that it was the Devil up to some hellish mischief, and ran for the priest. It happened that this was a particularly lazy priest, who had complained for years about pains in his legs, and who had himself carried to church on Sundays in a chair set on two stout carrying poles. Hearing about the Devil in the charnel house, he got all his holy paraphernalia together, and ordered four peasants to take him to the graveyard. The sexton walked beside him, carrying the sprinkler and the jug with the holy water.

Meanwhile the happy dimwit had worked hard all night. He was quite black with sweat and white with the dust of all the crumbling bones that had been piled in there for many generations. When the priest's procession got to the cemetery, and he stuck his head out of the charnel house, he looked like the Devil.

"Bring him over here, lads!" he shouted to the peasants, thinking that they were carrying a corpse. "And I'll fix him too!"

The peasants dropped the chair with the priest on the ground and took to their heels, with the sexton galloping right behind them. The priest, seeing that this was no joke but the real thing, got up on his own two feet and ran like a hare to the parish house, and from that time on nobody needed to carry him to church.

When the smiling dimwit came home, his brothers asked if he hadn't been afraid of the ghost in the charnel house that everybody talked about for years.

"Ghost?" he asked. "What's a ghost? I'll go look for one if you want. In fact I won't come home without one."

He set out that day and asked about a ghost everywhere he went. He came eventually to a large estate whose owner lived in a peasant hut right next to his castle because nobody could stand the noisy ghosts that haunted his ancestral home.

"I'll try it for a night," said the foolish lad. "Maybe I can stand it."

The lord of the manor advised him against it, but he pleaded so earnestly to be allowed to spend a night with ghosts, that he was given enough torches to last until morning, and then he was led to the haunted castle.

At about eleven o'clock that night, a great noise filled the castle, and soon afterwards a whole quarter of a human body tumbled in through the chimney. Then another quarter came flying in, followed by another, and then the rest of a man who had been hanged, drawn and quartered arrived in a heap. Devils appeared a few moments later, dressed like executioners, and started sharpening their knives and hooks and other instruments of torture while the miller's son watched them with great interest.

Then the Devils piled all the pieces of human flesh together, the body grew immediately into a complete man, and as the clock struck midnight it began to groan and move on the floor. But the foolish youth didn't think it right for a man to lie on the floor when he should be sitting, so he jumped up, picked up the apparition and seated it firmly on a stool beside the fireplace.

"Hey," he said after a while as he sniffed the air. "You don't smell too well. What's the matter with you?"

And then he slapped the ghost, on both cheeks, like his brothers did to him when he did something wrong.

But the apparition didn't mind at all. The Devils fled at once, howling in disappointment, but the ghost rose and thanked the grinning dimwit for saving his soul and giving him the peace of a quiet grave.

"I used to be the owner of this castle," he confessed. "I was a cruel master, stealing from the people, but I died unpunished. So I was doomed to stay on here as a ghost and to be hanged, drawn and quartered every night until the end of time, or until I was punished by a human hand.

"Moreover," he went on, "the treasures I collected are still in this castle, and if I give them all to you it'll be like returning them to everyone I wronged."

With this, the ghost took the miller's son into the lower dungeons, and then into an even lower cellar, and then into a third, and showed him the treasures. He told the lad how much should be given to the Church and how much he was to distribute among the poor.

"As for the rest," he said, "take it for yourself."

As always, the simple-minded lad did what he was told and became the richest man in the entire province. Wealth didn't change him. He stayed just as much of a dimwit as he had been before. But because he was very rich, everyone treated him with great respect and eventually he was elected to high provincial office.

His brothers no longer laugh at him today, and the ghost no longer haunts the castle.

About Two Brothers and the Spiteful Wife

THERE WERE ONCE TWO BROTHERS, one as rich as a peasant ever gets to be and the other poor, who lived next door to each other but hadn't seen each other for almost seven years. Perhaps the rich man would have been closer to his brother if his shrewish, spiteful and suspicious wife let him have his way.

It happened one day that the poor brother went to cut firewood in the forest. Since there was barely a handful of flour in his house to feed all his children, his wife gave him their last crust of bread and half a small cheese to last him until nightfall. He worked hard all day but he no sooner sat down to eat his meager supper when he saw a little man, dressed all in black, standing beside his cart.

"Let God bless those who share with others," said the little man.

"By all means," he said and invited the little man to join him. He then divided everything in two and shared it with the stranger.

"Because you gave me food," the little man told him, "you can have three wishes. Whatever you want to happen will happen. Just be sure to ask for what you really want, because three chances are all that anybody gets."

The poor woodcutter was a simple man. "I'll tell you what I really want," he said. "My sister-in-law is an angry, spiteful and malicious woman. She lives next door and she curses, chases and beats my children every time they come out into the yard. The first thing I'd want is for her to leave the kids alone and let me live in peace."

"Done," said the little man. "She won't bother you anymore after sundown tomorrow. Anything else?"

"I haven't seen my brother in close to seven years," the poor man sighed sadly. "Maybe he'd come over now and then if his wife would let him."

"He'll be knocking on your door this evening," the small magician said. "And what's your third wish?"

"Well, a few years ago I still had as much to live on as I needed. But all there's left today is an empty corn crib in the attic. If it's alright with you, I'd like it full of gold."

"If that's all, you can go home and start counting your money," the little man said and disappeared.

The poor man loaded his cart with firewood and drove it slowly home, and there his wife came out to greet him and help him stack the kindling in the woodshed.

"I think you and our poor children would like a good supper," the poor brother told her. "And I could do with a bite myself. Why don't you cook us something?"

"There's no more flour," she said, "and that's all we had."

"So go up to the attic, get a handful of gold ducats out of the old corn crib, change them at the tavern, and buy us a dinner. I wouldn't mind some beef, maybe a bit of veal, some fresh bread, some beer, and a little vodka."

His wife stood as if turned to stone, looking at her husband as if he'd gone mad. "Did you fall out of the cart and land on your head?" she asked. "What would gold be doing in that crib? There's not a copper penny anywhere in the house!"

But he just told her to do as he said, and to humor him, she went. She was back, however, in less time than it takes to say a Hail Mary, with a whole pile of shining golden ducats clutched against her breast, and eyes as big as saucers. She picked three ducats out of all that treasure, put her oldest child in the cart to help her, and drove to the market. But her suspicious sister-in-law watched her through the fence and ran to her own husband.

"Your brother's wife just put her oldest in the cart and drove away," she said with satisfaction. "Maybe she has left him?"

"Why should she do that?" asked the poor man's brother.

"Because he's poor and can't support his family," she replied with malicious pleasure. "I'll send our own children out into the yard to watch for her return, but I'll bet she is gone for good."

Half an hour later the poor man's wife was back, and the children of her spiteful neighbor watched in amazement as she carried a whole quarter of beef, another of veal, many loaves of bakery bread, many bottles of beer and a quart of vodka into her husband's house.

"I can't believe this!" cried their mother as soon as they told her. "Where would she get the money?" And then she sent her children to creep up to her neighbor's window and listen to what was being said inside.

Meanwhile the brother who had once been poor, but who was now richer than he knew, sent his wife next door to borrow a bushel basket, used to measure grain, so that he might start counting his money.

"They don't have any corn!" the spiteful woman cried out to her husband. "Their corn crib is empty! What could they be measuring?"

In the meantime, her brother-in-law had counted out fourteen bushel baskets of pure golden coins, and sent back the basket by one of his children. Peering inside, his rich brother noticed something gleaming at the bottom, pulled out his knife and pried out a ducat.

"They're counting gold by the bushel," he said to his wife, meaning it as a joke, but she said at once the coin must be stolen. Green with envy, and quite beside herself with rage, she was about to send for the magistrate, but her husband caught another gleam of gold in the bushel basket, knocked it against a wall, and watched, amazed, as fourteen newly-minted ducats fell out from between the plaited strips of wicker where they had been caught.

"My God, they *are* counting gold by the bushel!" cried his envious wife. "They must have murdered someone!"

The rich man ran at once to his brother. "You should take better care when you're counting money," he told him, more to draw him out than to give him warning. "I found these fourteen ducats caught in the wicker basket."

"Keep them," his brother said. "I have plenty more. God has provided everything I will ever need."

"How did he do that?" the rich brother demanded, and heard the whole story. Moreover, he followed the newly-rich woodcutter up into the attic where he could see the gold in the corn crib for himself.

"He must have made a deal with the Devil!" his wife said at once when told her what he had seen and heard.

"Impossible!" he told her. "He's too good and simple for anything like that."

"Well," she said spitefully, "God doesn't give that much for half a crust of bread and a bite of cheese."

Next day the rich brother set out into the forest to see if he could also meet the small magician and get three wishes for himself as well. His wife gave him a huge loaf of bread and two whole cheeses to share, although she didn't believe a word of his brother's story. After he piled his cart with firewood, as his brother had done, he sat down with his bread and cheeses and the little man in black appeared beside him.

"Let God bless those who share with others," he said as before.

"By all means," the rich man said, just like his once-poor brother. But when it came to naming his three wishes, he was afraid to say something that would anger his spiteful and suspicious wife so he asked if he could first talk it over with her.

"Go ahead," said the small magician. "And you don't even have to come back here to tell me your choice. Whatever three things you ask for at home before sundown will come true at once."

But the man's spiteful wife scoffed at him when he got back home and told her what happened.

"A likely story!" she snorted in contempt. "But let's test it out. You know that brindle cow of ours that broke her horn last summer? Let's wish for it to grow back."

Afraid to anger her, even though she was about to waste a good wish, the husband agreed. But they had no sooner made that foolish wish when a maid ran in from the byre to say that a beautiful new horn had grown on the brindle cow's head. They went at once to see it but the spiteful and suspicious wife still wouldn't believe it.

"I bet it'll fall right off when I twist it," she said, wrenched at the cow's new horn and broke it off again.

"Blast it!" cried the exasperated man. "That horn had no sooner grown back on the cow then you had to go and break it off! I wish it would grow on your head, you suspicious shrew!"

He no sooner spoke when the horn sprouted out of the middle of his wife's forehead, but no matter how they tugged and wrenched at it they couldn't break it off. The whole village came running to see this strange sight but no one had any advice to offer.

The sun was nearing the horizon then, and the wretched rich man had only one wish left before the end of day. "What shall it be?" he asked his wife. "Fame? Wealth? Power? Happiness? It's the last chance we have."

"I wish that cursed horn would fall off!" she shrieked, and that was their last wish.

The horn fell off. But the rich brother lost his mind with rage, thinking about all the treasures that he didn't get because of his shrewish, spiteful and suspicious wife, went to the forest and hanged himself. In despair, his wife jumped into the deepest well in the village and that was the end of her.

As for the woodcutter who had once been poor, he lived in peace and plenty until the end of his days with his wife and children, and everyone spoke highly of him as a generous friend who wasn't afraid to share his last crust of bread.

Three Brothers

THERE WAS ONCE a witch who had three lovely daughters and who was just as evil as her girls were good. She kept them in a castle deep inside the earth, and amused herself by flying around at night, disguised as a falcon, and knocking out the windows in the village churches.

It just so happened that three strong young brothers lived in the village she visited most often and they decided to get rid of the destructive bird one way or another. The two older brothers spent night after night in ambush with their bird guns, but the witch always threw a cloud of sleep on them before she appeared, and they woke only after hearing the sound of broken glass from the shattered windows.

When this had happened every night for a month or so, the youngest of the three suspected it was witchcraft and looked for a way to stay awake on watch no matter what happened. The idea came to him in church, when he looked at the figure of Jesus in his crown of thorns, and with his head dangling on his chest as if he were sleeping. He fixed a collar of thorns to his hunting shirt, right under his chin, thinking that the sharp spikes would wake him once he started nodding like his older brothers, and that's just what happened.

The moon had already risen, lighting up the night, when he heard a sound of wings hissing through the air and saw a great falcon swooping upon the church. But the witch also caught sight of him and threw a thick cloud of sleep over him, so that he closed his eyes and plunged into a dream. His head, however, had no sooner slumped across his shoulder when it struck a thorn, and the sharp pain brought him awake at once. He seized his bird gun, brought it to his shoulder, took aim at the falcon, and with the sound of the shot the bird plunged to earth with a broken wing. It hit the ground near a huge boulder but when the lad ran up to the great stone the wounded bird was gone.

What he found instead was that the earth had split where the bird had landed, and that a dark, deep pit had opened up just beside the boulder. He woke his brothers and they came running with a long, knotted rope and a bundle of tarred willow torches.

"If it's true what people say about the falcon being a witch," he told them, "and that she keeps three beautiful daughters in a golden castle deep inside the ground, then lower me into this hole and I'll send up whatever treasure I come across below."

His two brothers tied him quickly to the knotted rope, handed him the torches, and lowered him carefully into the deep dark hole. At first he could see nothing, and the smoking torches lit up only damp and dirty walls as he slid deeper and deeper into the black pit. Then, suddenly, he saw a beautiful landscape blooming at the bottom, with flowers that were fresh and new all the year round and trees that were always green. He saw a castle, built of brick and stone, with iron gates wide open as if to welcome him inside, and in a great hall, sheeted throughout in copper, he found a beautiful girl combing her golden hair.

Each hair that fell to the copper floor jingled like a coin, and she was so pretty and so well made, with bright, clear eyes and skin as white as the down on the breast of a swan, that the brave young man fell in love with her and asked her to marry him at once. She said she would as soon as they were both up on earth again, but warned him that he would never be able to return until he killed the falcon, who was her wicked mother.

"The only weapon that can kill the witch is a great sword that hangs in my sister's room in the castle tower," she told her young lover. "But it's so heavy that you'll never lift it."

The young man, however, wasn't the kind that gives up just because someone tells him something can't be done. He went deeper into the magic castle, entered a silver chamber in which sat the witch's second daughter, combing her silver hair. Each time one of the hairs fell to the silver floor it sounded like the plucked string of a violin.

She handed him the sword but he couldn't lift it, so he went in search of the oldest daughter, who also was a witch, but unlike her mother. Her spells and potions did no harm to people unless they were evil. She handed him three vials of a magic drink that would make him stronger, and he returned to the sword that could kill the mother.

One vial wasn't enough to lift the great weapon, no matter how he heaved and strained, so he drank another. This time he got it off the ground but only a little. The third vial, however, was enough. He swung the sword high into the air, hid in the castle courtyard, and waited for the falcon witch to come flying home.

She did at twilight, just before the dawn when all the ghosts and evil spirits come back to their graves. She flew in as the falcon, perched in a tree that gave golden apples, helped herself to a few and jumped to the ground. The moment that her feet touched the soil she turned into a woman and that was the moment for which the young man waited. He swung the sword, hit her in the neck, and the witch's head flew right off her shoulders.

Then, free of fear, he packed up all the treasures into many coffers which his two older brothers hauled up on their rope.

After that it was the turn of the three young women to rise to the surface and soon their brave young rescuer was left quite alone. There were no treasures left anywhere around him. He had sent up everything to his older brothers. But it occurred to him that such great riches might prove too much for them, and that they might be seized with greed and try to keep his share. Unlike his brothers, he had seen a bit of the world and learned not to trust everyone entirely.

To test them, he tied a boulder to the end of the knotted rope and shouted to his brothers to haul him to the surface. At first they pulled the rope steadily enough. But when the boulder rose halfway up the pit down which he had come, they suddenly let go. The boulder whistled down towards the bottom, struck the granite floor, and shattered into dust.

"That's how my bones would have shattered," the young man said sadly.

He wept a little for a while then, less for the treasures he had lost and even less for this proof of his brothers' treachery, than for the loss of the beautiful young woman with the swan's down skin and the golden hair.

He wandered far and long in that sunny country, deep under the ground where it was always spring, until he met another sorcerer who asked him why he was so downcast and alone. The young man told him his tale of faith, hope, courage, sudden treasures, love and treachery, and the sorcerer told him not to worry any more about it.

"I'll help to get you out of here if you help me," he said, since one good turn always deserves another. "My children are in danger from another sorcerer, who creeps about disguised as a giant worm and always wants to eat them. I've tried everything I know. I've hidden them in stone castles on the highest mountains, and here under the ground as well, but it's all for nothing. That great worm is just too much for me. Now I hid my little ones in the tree that bears the golden apples but that evil worm will get even there. Hide under that tree with your sword tonight, wait for my enemy who will come at midnight, cut off his head, and I will take you up on earth at once."

The youth agreed, climbed into the tree, picked some golden apples and had a healthy meal.

Right on the stroke of midnight a vast wind swept through all that country and the brave young man heard the rustling sound of something crawling up the apple tree. He looked down through the leaves and saw a huge white worm, as long and thick as the steeple of his village church, and with a head as vast as the boulder where the falcon fell after he had shot it, winding around the apple tree and creeping ever closer.

The sorcerer's children wept and huddled together in terror in the nest that their father built for them among the golden branches, and the great worm raised its massive head to search for them with its huge, flashing eyes, and its gaping jaws.

Then the young man swung his heavy sword, cut off the worm's head with a single stroke, chopped the great body into little pieces, and threw them to the four winds which howled overhead.

The father of the children, delighted to be rid of his enemy at last, took the lad on his shoulders just as he had promised, and carried him at once back to his old village.

There, however, everything was changed. His brothers had announced to everyone that he was dead and shared his treasures between them and lived like great lords. Each of them married one of the witch's daughters but made his own beloved, the beautiful girl with the golden hair, into their cook and her sisters' servant. They didn't recognize him when he ran into the hall of their manor house, but she knew immediately who he was and greeted him with cries and tears of joy.

"You thought you killed me," the young man told his frightened brothers. "But all you dropped and shattered was a stone. I'm here now, brought back by magic powers, and I want only what is mine."

Terrified, because they thought that the young man must have become a powerful magician, the brothers brought him everything he'd sent from the castle, fled with their wives and hid in the forest, but he ordered them found and brought back at once.

"Why can't we live together in peace," he asked, "like we did before? Must we be greedy and cold-hearted because we are rich? Take back your shares. There is enough for all. What happened in the past, belongs to the past and it has nothing to do with the here and now. Let's love each other like we did before I found these treasures and we'll be all the richer for having shared them fairly."

All of them fell into each other's arms and each forgave the other, and then the brave young man married the girl with the golden hair and went with her into the wide world.

He built her a castle with golden window frames, a silver roof and doors of beaten copper, and they lived there in happiness and plenty until the day he died.

The Tale of the Bad Brother

TWO BROTHERS ONCE LIVED in a little town. One, the older, was rich and selfish about his money, and the other was poor although he always tried to help everyone around him. The poor man often asked his brother for a little help, and one day when he came again, his brother told his wife: "I've had enough of this! I'm going to put out his eyes so that he can make a living begging on the highways."

Then he did as he said, although the poor brother pleaded and begged for mercy, and led him to the wayside shrine where many people passed each day to go to the market. He was about to leave him there when he remembered all the money he had given to him in the past and took him, instead, to the gallows where no one ever came. The blind man cried and pleaded all day, thinking that pious travelers would be sure to take pity on him and help him, but there was nobody to hear him and no one gave him alms. He didn't know where he was. He didn't know if it was night or day until he heard the town clock strike eleven times and half an hour later three Devils flew in and settled on the gallows in the form of ravens.

"What trouble can we cause tonight?" one asked, and another said: "There's a woman in the next village who just had a baby and she's laid up in bed. Her husband works hard all day and he doesn't get home until late at night, while her kitchen wench has the habit of leaving as soon as she's cooked supper, so there's no one to say 'God bless you' to her when she sneezes. We could rip out the bottom log in one of the walls and carry her off along with her baby."

"People are so blind," laughed the other Devil. "You know that town three miles away where there is no water? The people have to walk all day to the river for a bucketful and they curse the trip every step of the way. They had well-diggers working all month in the market square but they've hit a rock and they've given up. If they'd just lift that rock they'd hit the best spring

65

in the country. We could lift up that rock ourselves and drown the whole town unless somebody threw a quilt over the well to quieten the water, but nobody would ever think of something like that."

"The lady of the manor at Paprociny will soon be ours to take," the third Devil said. "She's been sick seven years and no doctors can cure her. What they don't know is that she once spat out a communion wafer and a toad swallowed it. That toad is sitting under her kitchen cupboard, and all that needs to be done is to cut it open, take out and wash the wafer and give it to her again, and she'd be up and around in three days. But nobody would ever think of that so she'll soon be dead."

Not to be outdone, the first Devil said: "You're right about people being blind. This country is full of blind beggars begging at the shrines, but all of them would get their sight back if they knew how to go about it. There's a certain root that grows under every gibbet, just like the one here, that can cure any kind of blindness. All you have to do is squeeze the juice out of it, rub it on your eyelids, and you'd see as clear as day even if you were blind from birth or had your eyes put out."

Then the clock struck midnight and the Devils flew off to do their night's mischief. The blind man groped around, soon discovered that he lay under a gibbet, not a wayside shrine, and started digging for the magic root. He found it deep under a clump of nettles, rubbed it on his eyelids, and his eyesight started coming back at once. By dawn he could see everything around him even better than he could see before and set out to find the house of the woman who just had the baby. He found it close to sundown and asked her for a place to sleep.

"You won't sleep well here," she said. "My baby's restless and cries a lot. You'd do better next door at my neighbor's who doesn't have small children. Besides, I've caught a cold and I sneeze a lot."

"I'd rather stay here with you," the poor man said and found a stool near the woman's bed where he could keep watch. "At least I'd be able to say 'God bless you' when you sneeze."

Just then the kitchen wench brought in a pot of soup, threw the spoons on the table and walked out without a word, and the bedridden woman sneezed.

"God bless you!" the poor man cried quickly and, at once, there was a frightful roar outside, the walls shook and all the holy pictures came tumbling to the floor, because the Devils were already wrestling with the floor-beams. The master of the house came running in, just as terrified as everybody else, but the Devils were already gone by then, driven off by the poor man's blessing.

The grateful master poured gold into the poor man's pockets when he heard the story, and had him guided next morning to the town with the unfinished well, and there the good brother announced that he could make the water flow even though everyone said that the well was dry.

"You do that," said the mayor and the city council, "and we'll give you our water tax for the next ten years, because we're all sick of walking to the river every day."

The poor brother climbed into the wall with a pick and shovel and started to work. He had the big rock out of there in less than an hour, and a pure, fresh-water spring shot high into the air. There was so much water pouring out all at once that it looked as if it would flood the town, but the poor man ran into the nearest house, got a quilt, threw it across the top of the well, and the water soon quietened down again.

The mayor of the town was so delighted that he paid him a year's tax on account, and the poor brother bought himself a handsome cart and a pair of horses with which he rode to Paprociny where he passed the word that he could cure the sick lady of the manor.

"You do that," said the lord of the manor, "and I'll give you half of everything I own, because the doctors would take it all for nothing anyway."

The new healer ordered the huge kitchen cupboard moved aside, caught the toad sitting under it, cut it open and removed the communion wafer, then washed it and gave it to the sick woman to swallow properly, which she did at once even though she was very close to dying. But in only an hour she sat up and called for a hearty supper, and two mornings later she was up and around and walking about outside.

The lord of the manor was overjoyed and immediately signed over half of his estates to the miracle worker who went back to his relatives not only rich but famous.

"You wanted to harm me, brother," he said when he got home, "but it all turned out better than I ever had before."

The bad brother turned green with envy at all this good fortune. "Do for me what I had done to you," he begged, "and lead me to that gallows."

The younger brother didn't want to hurt the older for all the riches in the world, but the greedy, envious man insisted, telling him it was his duty to share his good fortune, so he blinded him and led him to the gibbet. The rich, blinded man sat there all alone until the clock in the town struck eleven times and the three Devils flew in as before.

"Something's wrong," said the first. "Everything we've planned has fallen apart. They've saved the bedridden woman and the baby. The city people have a good new well and no longer curse every day as they go to the river. The lady of Paprociny has never been healthier. I haven't seen such bad luck since I became a Devil."

"Somebody must be spying on us and learning all our secrets," said the second Devil.

He jumped down, started to sniff around and soon found the blinded rich man sitting in the nettles.

"Here he is!" he shouted. "Now we'll pay him back!"

The other two Devils hopped down at once, leaped on the bad brother and tore him to pieces, and that was his reward for lack of charity and compassion, and for all his envy, selfishness and greed.

About Mat the Fool and How He Used His Head

THERE WAS ONCE a shepherd living in a village who had two smart sons and one who wasn't smart at all. His name was Little Mat and all he liked to do was sleep by the stove and eat baked potatoes. His brothers always told him to learn to use his head but he had no idea how to go about it.

One day the shepherd had to go to market so his two older boys had to tend his flocks. Little Mat didn't want to go into the fields because that would take him away from his stove and his baked potatoes. But his mother woke him up, told him to take their dinner out to his two brothers, and gave him a basket. In it she put a bowl of poached noodles and a jug of buttermilk. Then she gave him a sack with a large loaf of bread.

"Take this to your brothers," she told Little Mat, "and try to use your head along the way."

Mat took careful note of what his mother said and set out at once for the shepherds' meadow. But just beyond the fence was a ditch and the bridge across it had a hole in it. Mat thought he might fall through the hole and break a leg, in which case he wouldn't get to the shepherds' pasture, but he remembered what his mother told him. "I don't know how to use my head," he said to himself. "But this big round loaf might do just as well."

So he plugged the hole in the bridge with the loaf of bread, hopped across it, and looked back to see if he hadn't fallen in after all. But what he saw instead was his own dark shadow.

"What's that?" he cried out. "Maybe that's a Devil that's trying to eat me!"

He ran for his life, leaping across ditches and tripping in the furrows, and kicking up a huge cloud of dust. But whenever he looked back there was the dark shadow running at his heels.

"Everybody's always telling me to use my head," he said to the shadow, "so here's an idea. Why eat me when you can have buttermilk and noodles?"

And he began throwing noodles and spooning buttermilk back across his shoulders to feed the hungry Devil at his heels until everything was gone.

"Where's our dinner, dimwit?" his brothers shouted when he handed them the empty basket.

"He took it," Mat said and pointed at his shadow. "This Devil was chasing me and wanted to eat me so I fed him the noodles and buttermilk instead."

But this infuriated his hungry brothers even more. "That's your shadow, idiot! Why don't you use your head?"

"Shadow?" Mat wondered. "What's a shadow? So why didn't you tell me about it before? If you had, I'd have known how to use my head and you'd have your dinner."

But what difference does an explanation make when a man is hungry? The shepherds left Little Mat in charge of the sheep while they went home to dinner.

"Keep them clubbed close together in a bunch so they don't wander off," they said as they left. "And try to use your head."

Little Mat paid close attention to everything they said, determined to use his head at last. He cut a thick cudgel off a tree, began to club the straying sheep until he killed about half of them, and then he piled them on top of each other in what he thought looked like a tidy bunch.

When his two brothers were on their way back from their dinner he ran out to meet them. "Look how well I tend sheep!" he cried. "I've clubbed them like you said and they're all bunched together."

But they began to shout at him at once: "What a misfortune you are to us, you bird-brain. When will you learn how to use your head?"

"Well," said Little Mat. "You should have told me beforehand about clubs and bunches. But I'll know better next time."

The smart brothers didn't know what to do about the dead sheep so Mat suggested they take them to the pen where they stayed at home. "We'll pile them in there and let people think a bear got in and killed them. Is this using my head?"

The brothers carried the sheep home two at a time but they loaded Little Mat down with four or more. Then they ran to hide in the forest before their father came home from the market. But they no sooner hid themselves when they remembered that they hadn't locked the gate to the sheepfold so they sent Little Mat running back to do it.

"Go back and get us something else to eat," they said, "and then lock and watch that gate so nobody will open it and come after us."

Little Mat trotted back to the village, picked some pears off his mother's tree and stole a jug of vinegar from the kitchen. But he didn't know how to bring the food to the forest and watch the sheepfold gate at the same time.

"I guess I still haven't learned how to us my head," he told himself sadly, so he took the gate off its hinges, loaded it with the vinegar and the apples, and carried them all on his back to where his brothers waited.

"Now we can watch the gate right here," he told them, "and if anybody tries to open it we can chase him off."

"Oh what a fool you are!" complained the smart brothers. "What use will you ever be to anybody with a head like yours?"

But now they knew that they had to run away from home because their father would skin their tails for them once he found the dead sheep in the open sheepfold, so they plunged deep into the forest.

"Since you brought the gate," they told Little Mat, "you can carry it the rest of the way. And if it's too heavy for your back, put it on your head!"

Mat did as he was told, but he loaded the jug of vinegar and the bag of pears on top of the gate before he hefted them to the top of his toussled mop of hair.

"Now I'm finally using my head for something," he said to his brothers. "But I can't carry the gate and the rest as well, so let the gate carry half the load."

But the smart brothers didn't want to talk to him any more. They walked all day deep into the forest and at dusk they climbed into a tall pine and tried to go to sleep. However, they were no sooner hidden in the branches when they heard a loud noise below and saw six men, each broad as a barn door with long black beards dangling on their chests, and even longer knives stuck into the belts. Even Little Mat knew that they were bandits and all three brothers started to sweat in fear.

The bandits settled below them for the night, lit a big bonfire and spitted some venison for roasting, and the heat of the fire made the hidden shepherds sweat harder than ever. But Little Mat sweated even more because he still had the heavy gate on top of his head.

"Those pears are getting heavy," he whispered to his brothers. "I'm going to let them drop."

They pleaded with him to hang onto them, or they'd be sure to give them all away, but the pears were already dropping through the branches.

"That's odd," the robbers peered uneasily at each other. "Pinecones are falling on us though there's no wind to shake them."

The gate, however, weighed terribly on Mat who thought that it was the jug of vinegar that was so awfully heavy.

"I'm going to drop the jug," he told his frightened brothers and let it go even before they could beg him to hang onto it. On its way down, the jug got caught in some of the branches and the vinegar spilled on the highwaymen below.

"There's something wrong here," they muttered to each other. "It's close to midnight but the dew is falling as if it was dawn. Maybe the Devil is after us at last for all the terrible crimes we've done all these years."

Just then Mat dropped the gate and it came crashing down through the branches and the superstitious bandits leaped up in terror.

"The Devil's here!" they shouted.

They ran for their lives, having much to answer for to the Devil. But one of them was lame and didn't get away before the gate hit him on the head and slammed his mouth shut just as he had stuck his tongue between his teeth.

"Wait for me-e-e!" he shouted to the others, but with his tongue cut off it sounded like 'Fle-e-e,' and the whole band ran off all the faster.

When all the robbers disappeared, the three brothers climbed down to the bonfire and had a good meal because the bandits left everything behind when they ran away. They also left two big sacks of gold they'd stolen on the highways, which the three lads took home to buy their father a new flock of sheep.

"Where did this come from?" their parents asked, amazed, and were even more astonished when the two smart brothers told them that it was all the work of Little Mat who had finally learned how to use his head.

More than a sack and a half of gold was left after they bought the new flock of sheep, so they got themselves a big new house, clothes of the finest silk, and bright new kerchiefs for their mother to wear to church on Sundays. They dressed Little Mat in a fancy frock coat like a wise professor, and in shiny shoes and stocking such as women wear. But for all this finery he remained their dumb Little Mat, who went on sleeping by the stove and eating baked potatoes, which he is probably doing to this day.

Of Argelus and the Swans

THERE WAS ONCE a king whose oldest son was such a beautiful young man that he lived in a separate castle of his own to save him from the temptations of the court. His name was Argelus. His father loved him more than anything. But because he cared for him so much, and worried so much about him, the king wouldn't let him go anywhere, not even outside his castle gates, in case some evil breeze should brush against him and do him some harm.

"Never, never take any risks," he told him. "Never leave your castle grounds and never go out at night."

The young prince could have anything he wanted except the freedom to try something new, and though the king himself came often to see him, he was bored with life and longed for an adventure.

Then something happened. One day a strange tree sprung up in his gardens. It bore fresh golden blossoms every morning and golden fruit at night. The king was delighted with this tree and called on all the most notable peers of the realm to come and look at it, and to make sure the fruit wouldn't be stolen, as sometimes happens at night even among princes, he put a guard around it. But though the sentries didn't take their eyes off that tree all night, all the fruit had disappeared by morning.

The king doubled the guard but the same thing happened the next night and the next as well. Each dawn fresh golden blossoms bloomed on all the branches, each evening golden fruit hung where the blooms had been, but by first light all of them were gone.

Puzzled, the king called on his court magician to supply an answer.

"I'll tell you, Sire," the famous wizard said, "but you'll kill me for it."

"Nonsense," said the king. "Speak up, solve this riddle, and you won't be sorry."

"There's only one man in this kingdom who can guard that tree," the

73

magician said. "That's Argelus, your son. Send him out tonight to watch in the gardens and all will be well."

"What?" the furious king could hardly believe his ears. "You'd expose Argelus to some dangerous adventure? He might catch a cold! A vampire might bite him! Guards! Take this lying old man out of here and cut off his head!"

The king had another son whom he didn't like because the lad was always up to mischief, taking risks as if he lived by them, but he allowed the boy to guard the tree that night, thinking that if the sentry had to be a prince this lad would do as well as Argelus.

The madcap prince, however, did no better than the common sentries. He watched all night. He never blinked an eye. But in the morning all the fruit was gone. Angry about that, he told the whole story to Argelus who seized on it as a chance for an adventure. When the king came to see him later in the day Argelus put on a long face and sighed as if troubled.

"What's wrong?" cried the king, alarmed and thinking that Argelus must be ill?

"Ah, it's nothing, father," Argelus replied. "I had a dream about that marvelous tree in our gardens. It seems that I'm the only one who is able to guard it. That makes it my duty. But since you won't let me out at night I think I'll just put a knife to my throat and be done with it."

"Don't even think about that!" cried the king. "Alright! You can guard the tree. But wrap yourself up well against the night chill and watch out for anything that might harm you."

Argelus ordered his bed, a table and some lamps placed under the tree, and took along a servant he thought he could trust. He stretched out on the bed with a book to keep himself awake. At midnight, seven swans flew in and settled in the tree and Argelus reached up as far as he could, caught one and brought it down. The swan immediately turned into a beautiful young woman, an enchanted princess, and the remaining six turned into her handmaidens.

"What an adventure!" Argelus was delighted, and the princess begged him to spend three nights on guard at the tree, and never close an eye, because that was the only way to break the spell she was under.

At dawn the girls turned back into swans and flew away but this time all the golden fruit was left on the branches. The king was delighted. Argelus didn't tell him about the swan princess and swore his servant to secrecy as well. But this man was courting the daughter of a certain witch and told her all about it the very same day. She in turn told her mother. The mother saw a chance for mischief, the way some witches do, and gave the love-sick servant a bag full of dreams and a vial of special, aromatic oil.

"When Argelus lies down tonight," she told him, "Open this bag and he'll fall asleep at once. Then, when the swans fly away, smear some of this oil on each of his eyelids. He'll wake at once and think that he never closed an eye."

That night Argelus went on guard again, but as soon as the love-sick servant opened the bag of dreams, he fell asleep as suddenly and as totally as if someone had hit him with a hammer. The swans came as before, and turned into girls, but though the princess shook the sleeping Argelus as hard as she could, he couldn't be wakened. She even ordered the servant to awake his master but the man refused.

"Tell your master to keep better watch tomorrow night," the sad and disappointed princess told the servant. "Otherwise my spell will last another seven years."

Just before dawn the swans flew away. The disloyal servant rubbed the waking oil on his master's eyelids, Argelus awoke, and saw that the golden fruit had vanished as before. But he was far more angry at having missed the princess with whom he had fallen head-over-heels in love.

Once more he told the servant not to breathe a word about this to anyone but, once again, the servant told the witch who talked him into doing the same thing the next night.

Once more, Argelus fell asleep on guard. Once more the swans flew in, changed into girls, and tried to wake the prince. They even got him off his bed and walked him around, but nothing could break the sleep released by the bag of dreams. Once again the princess told the servant to caution his master that if he didn't stay awake at least one more night he'd never be able to free her from her spell and become her husband. The servant said all this to Argelus after he rubbed the waking oil on his eyes but he said nothing about the dream pouch or the witch.

Argelus tried to force himself to sleep all day so that he'd stay awake that night but it was all for nothing. Sleep overwhelmed him as before, and when the swan girls found no means to wake him, they told the servant that the prince would never see any of them again.

"And if your master wants to know the reason he failed us," the princess told the servant, "tell him to move the sword that hangs over his bed to another peg and he will know the truth. Now we must do the rest of our penance in the Black City, east of the sun and west of the moon."

Poor Argelus went back to his castle, along with the servant, and since the man had told him what the princess said, he took the sword that hung over his bed in the castle and moved it to another peg. The swordpoint immediately rose and pointed to the servant so that Argelus knew at once he had been betrayed. He seized the sword, cut off the false servant's head, and then told the whole story to his father. But the king wouldn't hear of letting him go to search for the swan princess he wanted to marry.

"There'll be risks," he said. "You will have adventures. Moreover, you'll learn things no prince or king should know."

True love, however, cannot be denied. Argelus wasted away to nothing in his grief and longing, so that the king, worried about his health, relented and let him go. He gave him coaches, horses, servants and all the money he might need to reach the Black City, and Argelus set out on his famous journey. He searched for the Black City in many distant lands, traveling seven years, until all his money was gone. Unable to pay his servants, he sent them all home. He had to trade his coaches and his horses for food and shelter as he traveled on, and then went on foot begging on the highways, so that he learned how common people live in worry and hunger, and his heart almost broke at the fate of the poor and homeless. He also learned that poor people must take devious paths just to stay alive.

One day he came across three youths who were fighting each other in a forest, although it was clear by the looks of them that all three were brothers.

"Our father left us only what you see right here," they told him. "A table, a whip, a saddle and a horse. We can't make up our minds how we should divide this because one thing depends upon the other and there's only one of us who could use it all."

The problem, they explained, was that their inheritance was magic.

"Whoever puts that saddle on that horse," they said, "then cracks that whip and names his destination, will be transported there at once. And then the horse, the saddle and the whip will come back to whoever hits that table with his fist."

"I am a royal prince," Argelus informed them. "Why don't you let me decide for you all?" Then he set them running all together to three equidistant mountains. "The first of you to come back here from the top of his mountain will get the whole inheritance," he said.

The brothers agreed and raced off at once but Argelus didn't wait for them. He saddled the magic horse with the magic saddle, mounted, cracked the magic whip, named his destination, and immediately flew several

hundred miles. But the three brothers returned long before he reached the Black City and started hammering the table in their rage. The horse immediately tossed Argelus into a great swamp and flew back to the brothers along with the saddle and the whip.

Argelus barely managed to save himself from drowning in the quagmire. He managed to crawl out, hungry and exhausted, and made his way to a nearby hut whose hospitable owner welcomed him, fed him a good supper, and offered sound advice.

"I've heard of the Black City," he told him. "But I don't know where it is, nor how far from here. But why don't you stay with me for a few days? Merchant caravans go by all the time, and so do people traveling to church festivals, and someone will be sure to tell you what you want to know."

Three caravans went by in as many days but no one had heard about the Black City. Finally, a passing stranger said that it lay 150 leagues to the east, and that he knew the way, but that he had business in the west and couldn't help Argelus much as he might want to. Argelus, however, still had one precious stone left of all his treasures and possessions. He gave it to the stranger so that he'd change his mind.

"Alright," the stranger said. "I'll go east with you and take you within sight of the Black City. But I've been outlawed from that place and it'll be my death if they catch me there. So once you've seen it on the horizon before you, you'll be on your own."

That's what they agreed to and that's what they did. Argelus had no more trouble with directions after that. He got to the Black City and spent several days wandering through the streets, trying to think where to start searching for the princess he loved so much and wanted to marry. Since seven years had passed from the moment he'd seen the swan maidens, he knew her spell must have ended by this time and he could ask her to become his wife.

But as he wandered through the streets he saw that the Black City was getting ready for a celebration. "Our king's daughter is marrying some foreign prince," he was told. "She had been under a spell for a while, living as a swan, but it's all over now and we'll be having a royal wedding next week."

Saddened to hear this, Argelus went at once to the royal castle but the guards wouldn't let him in. He looked so poor they took him for a beggar or, worse yet, for something that had just crawled out of a swamp.

Luckily, the princess sent one of her maidens to the town that day to buy her wedding gown. She still loved Argelus, whose beauty she couldn't forget, but since she never expected to see him again she agreed to marry another prince so that her country might have a ruler when her father died. Her messenger, however, was one of the girls who had been with her as a swan during her enchantment, and she saw and recognized Argelus at once.

Told about this, the princess couldn't believe it.

She sent another swan girl to make sure, and then she sent a third, but when all three swore that this was the same beautiful young man they had seen under the tree with the golden fruit, and that they remembered him too well to make a mistake, she went out to look for him herself.

What happened after that is known to one and all. They saw each other, fell in love all over again, married, had many children, and lived happily the rest of their lives. When the old king died, Argelus became the ruler of the country. And because he had learned in his journeys what few kings or princes ever hear about, and saw for himself how poor people live, he was a good and fair king loved by everyone.

The Sorcerer's Apprentice

THERE WAS ONCE a poor cobbler who drank up everything he earned so that his wife and family were always in need. His daughters long gave up any thought of dowry, and the family's only hope was the shoemaker's young son. He was a bright, shrewd lad who knew how to take care of himself in the world, so his mother decided to apprentice him to some master craftsman.

One day, when he was already in his teens, she dressed him as handsomely as she could, pressed him to her heart, combed his hair neatly, took him to church where they said a prayer, and then set out with him on a long journey to the capital where he'd be able to learn an honest trade. They were about halfway there when a strange nobleman, dressed in a black cape, sprung out of nowhere.

He liked the looks of the smart, sprightly lad, as the good woman could see with her mother's eye, and argued with her for an hour and more to let him have the boy as an apprentice. But since he neither greeted her with *'Praised be the Lord Jesus Christ,'* nor told her what trade he represented, and since he didn't look right to her anyway, she tried to put him off. Finally, when he refused to give up and kept pressing her to give him the boy, she snapped at him to leave them both alone, and they walked away.

But they hadn't gone many miles when they found themselves in a strange, empty wilderness, with neither a village nor an inn anywhere in sight, and where they met no living creature the rest of the day. The sun was so hot in that unknown country, and they walked so far since they left their home, that they were soon exhausted by thirst, heat and hunger and sat down hopelessly in the sandy road.

Worried about the boy, the mother burst into helpless tears, and he sniffed a little in his own turn, worried about her, and at once a large boulder leaped out of the ground beside them. Standing on top of it was a silver platter with a steaming roast, a loaf of white bread and a jug of beer. The travelers rushed eagerly to the boulder, but when they stretched their hands towards this providential supper it vanished, leaving only the bare boulder in the heat and sand. As soon as they walked away from it, however, the nourishment reappeared as before!

This happened several times. The food was there when they couldn't reach it, and gone when they could. The sight of it only added to their thirst and hunger as if someone wanted to tease them on purpose. The smart boy guessed at once what this was all about, snapped a length off his aspen walking staff, and plunged it like a stake into the ground where the rock's shadow fell.

The rock disappeared at once. In its place stood the same black-caped noble they had met before, with the aspen stake driven through his cloak, pinning him to the ground. He whined and squirmed as if someone had thrown boiling water over him, and he was so shrunken and disheveled in his misery, that the good woman almost took pity on the sorcerer and pulled up the stake, but the smart lad stopped her just in time.

"I've got you now!" he told the pleading sorcerer. "And I won't set you free until we make a deal. You've led us to this desert and you've had your fun. So now you can stand here for a year and six weeks, or until you've dried up like that stake with which I've pinned you to the ground."

"Have mercy, young master," begged the trapped magician. "Ask me for anything you want if you set me free!"

"So be it," said the boy. "First, turn into that rock again and make sure all the food is on it as before."

The black-caped noble vanished and the boulder stood in his place again, along with the silver platter, the roast, the bread and the beer. The boy and his mother had a hearty dinner, thanked God for his mercy, and the sorcerer reappeared again.

"Well, lad," he whined. "What about that stake?"

"Not so fast, good master!" cried the boy. "I'll let you go if you take me on as an apprentice for three years, which is what you wanted in the first place. And to make sure you teach me all your magic, I'll take some gold right now to prove your good intentions."

The sorcerer bent down, kicked up some sand from under his feet and poured a handful of gold ducats into the boy's cap.

"Fine," said the boy. "That'll take care of mother while I am away. But a piece of your own ear would give me some power over you, and that's what I need to take care of me."

"Oh alright," the magician shrugged and thrust his right ear towards the waiting boy. "Have a piece of this one."

"Hmm," said the lad. "You're a bit too willing to give me your right ear so I'll take the left one."

With this he caught the sorcerer by the nose, turned his head around, and nicked a slice out of his left ear, which is the one that counts when it comes to magic because it's closer to the heart. Then he folded it in half and put it away in his traveling bag, made a sign of the cross over it and pulled the aspen stake out of the ground.

The sorcerer groaned, rubbed his wounded ear, stood on his head, squawked like a chicken and turned into a rooster, but it was a rooster as big as a horse and as black as the magician's cape.

"You drive a hard bargain," he said to the lad. "So that's one thing I don't have to teach you. Now, take your mother home and come to the crossroads at midnight. I'll pick you up there and keep you for three years."

With this he cawed like a crow, turned into a raven, flapped his wings three times and disappeared.

The boy did just what his new master told him, poured all the gold he'd been given into his mother's apron, kissed her hands, and asked her to come for him in three years to the same spot where they left the sorcerer. It was a wilderness, sure enough, but he thought his home had to be somewhere there.

"I think he'll try to trick us in some way," he warned her, "so he can keep me the rest of my life, but maybe I'll learn enough in the next three years to turn the tables on him."

Then he hugged his old mother once again, asked for her blessing, and got to the crossroads at the appointed time. But midnight came and went and the sorcerer failed to appear.

The lad stood leaning for a while on a broken sign-post, which pointed straight down into the ground, then put the slice of the magician's ear in his teeth and bit hard on it. At once, the roadsign howled in pain and swayed from side to side, and the boy just had time to leap out of the way, and to read the inscription which said *'To the Devil,'* when the post was gone and the sorcerer was there.

"To the Devil," the boy read out again, then asked: "Would that be you yourself, Master Sorcerer?"

"I wouldn't be at all surprised," groaned the dark-cloaked noble. "But what are you biting me for? I'm here, aren't I? Ah, what am I going to do with you, anyway? Oh, alright, let's go then. I'll take you home for an education.

But remember that you're now my student. You'll do what you're told and you'll stay with me until your mother comes and takes you home."

That's how the cobbler's son become the sorcerer's apprentice. He stayed the full three years. In that time he learned everything there was to know about the black arts until he knew as much as his master. He learned how to turn himself inside out and then back again. He knew how to change into any animal or bird, and how to fly to the moon and back, and how to plait a buggy-whip out of sand. Many parents apprenticed their children to this magician because he was also a master alchemist, and knew how to turn base metals into gold, but he'd always trick them in some way when they came back for their sons or daughters so that they had to go home without them.

The bright lad watched and learned all the guessing games by which the sorcerer kept his apprentices past their appointed time, so that three days before his own mother was to come for him he went out to meet her and told her how to spot him among the illusions the sorcerer would create to fool her.

"Remember, mother," he said. "When he calls for a herd of horses, I'll be the one with a fly buzzing 'round my ear. If it's a flock of pigeons pecking at dry peas, I'll be the one that just pretends to eat. And if it's a circle of beautiful maidens, I'll have a ladybug just above my brow."

When the shoemaker's wife arrived at the magician's house and asked for her son, he took a copper trumpet off the wall and blew a fanfare to the four corners of the world. A herd of jet-black horses appeared suddenly in the sky and came to earth in a half-circle around the trembling woman. But these were not real horses, only the tricked apprentices the sorcerer had stolen from their parents.

The worried woman went from horse to horse, hoping her mother's heart would tell her which of them was her son, until she noticed a small fly buzzing around the ear of one of the horses.

"That's my son!" she cried out happily, but the magician only shrugged and reached for a silver trumpet.

This time, when he blew a blast to each of the four corners of the world, a flock of milk-white pigeons appeared around the woman and settled on the ground. They started pecking eagerly at the dried peas strewn throughout the courtyard, but one, she noticed, only pretended to gobble up the food.

"This is my boy!" she cried again, and pointed, and the magician got a bit annoyed.

"I don't know how you did that, woman," he said. "No other mother ever got this far. But this next test will stump you or you can live until you're a hundred."

With this he called to the four corners of the world with a golden trumpet, a strange melodious singing echoed in the air, and rows of beautiful girls began descending from the clouds in pairs. Each wore a dress as white as snow, with pink sashes around their waists and garlands of cornflowers in their hair, and they formed a singing circle around the wondering mother. Looking with care at each girl in turn, she went slowly from one to another until she found one with a tiny ladybug sitting on her eyebrow.

"And here he is again!" she cried out.

The magician cursed. The girls immediately turned into twittering sparrows and flew out of the window. One stayed behind, turned into his mother's son again, and threw himself gratefully at her feet and then into her arms.

They went home with joy. But the young man soon noticed that poverty had moved back in as well. The sorcerer's gold was long spent and the father sold or pawned everything else they had to keep on with his drinking and carousing.

"So there you are," he greeted the sorcerer's apprentice. "What have you learned in the last three years? And what kind of help can I expect from you?"

"I've learned how to do magic," the apprentice said. "And here's how I'll help you. I can change into any bird or animal you want, whether it's a falcon, a ram, a greyhound or a nightingale. You can sell me at the market and I'll come right home so you can sell me again in another form. Just make sure you always take the halter off me, and that you never ask me to become a horse. If I'm turned into a horse, you'll get no use out of the money you're paid, and something bad could happen to me as well."

The cobbler wanted a falcon to sell and, at once, there was a beautiful falcon sitting on his shoulder, complete with a handsome hood and a falconer's gauntlet in his beak. The shoemaker took him to town, sold him to some hunters, and found his son eating supper when he got back home.

When the shoemaker drank up all the money he got for the falcon, he asked for a greyhound, and a sleek greyhound was sitting at his feet the moment he said it. He took the dog by the collar, went back to the hunters, got good money for him, and again found his son at the supper table when he got back home. He was beside himself with joy, since he was now convinced that he'd never again run short of money for the finest vodka.

So the sorcerer's apprentice was sold as an ox, a milk-cow, a ram, a goose, a rooster and a turkey, but his father drank up the money faster than he could make it and he soon started to complain that he needed more.

"Why can't you be a horse?" he demanded. "People don't pay much for the farmyard animals you've been changing into. How much can I ask for just another chicken? But a horse would bring enough money to last me a week, and I'm tired of taking you to market every day."

The son told him never to ask for that and the shoemaker got angry. Why not? he asked himself. Who could stop him? And what harm could there be in it anyway? It was just his son's stubbornness and ill will, he thought, that was depriving him of quick money and a handsome profit.

So one day, when he was somewhat the worse for wear after a night's drinking, he ordered a horse, and a beautiful thoroughbred appeared right outside the window. His coat glistened, he pawed the ground with a strong leg, and it seemed as if he'd let sparks fly from his eyes and flames from his nostrils.

The cobbler rode off on the horse, found a buyer as soon as he got to town, and not just an ordinary buyer but a rich Armenian who said he'd buy the horse for his weight in gold. Anxious with sudden greed, the shoemaker backed the horse onto a set of scales, while gold ducats were poured straight out of their sacks into the other pan until their blinding glare began to hurt the eyes.

Up went the scale with the horse upon it, and down went the pan into which gold was being poured, and the shoemaker started thinking he had died and was now in heaven. But suddenly, when the scales hung balanced evenly in the air, the chains supporting them snapped apart, both the scales tilted, and all the gold ran down the sloping gutters to the river. The cobbler went running after the rolling ducats and quite forgot about the halter on the horse's neck. Indeed, he even forgot about the horse itself.

Meanwhile the Armenian stamped hard on the ground, changed into a laughing noble who wore a black cape, leaped onto the horse and galloped out of the town. He rowelled him mercilessly with his spurs, beat him with a whip and sawed on his bridle until the horse was bleeding, because this was the thwarted master sorcerer who wanted to pay his smart young apprentice for that nick in his ear.

When he had run the horse so hard that pink froth bubbled out of his gasping mouth, the sorcerer rode it to his invisible house. Although this house stood in the open, with magic gardens flowering all around it, it looked like an empty, barren wilderness to anyone who wasn't invited there, and though hundreds of travelers passed that way each year nobody knew where the magician lived.

The sorcerer tied the horse to the porch rail and went off to give orders to have the horse stabled in a cold, windy barn full of rats and spiders. Knowing what was in store for him, the poor horse tossed his mane, snagged the bridle on a nail in the hitching post, worked the halter off his head, stamped with all four hooves on the ground beneath him, changed into a hare and fled across the field. But the master sorcerer saw him through a window, changed into a hound, and streaked after him. He was about to clamp his teeth on the hare's tail when the hare bounced off a sloping hillside straight into the air, turned into a swallow and hid in the clouds.

Foiled, the hound changed into a hawk, shot high above the poor swallow and dived down upon it with talons spread wide, when the swallow skimmed the waves of a great lake and turned into a guppy that hid in the grasses at the water's edge. But at that moment the hawk dived into the lake and became a pike that went after the guppy. It was about to crush the poor guppy in its cruel jaws when the guppy gathered its last strength, flipped out of the water and turned into a golden ring that fell at the feet of a beautiful princess who was resting on the lakeshore after bathing there. She was the daughter of a mighty prince who ruled that whole country. She caught the ring, slipped it on her finger and looked about with delight and wonder.

Meanwhile the foiled sorcerer stepped out of the lake in the form of a goose, shook off the drops of water that clung to his back, and turned into a Greek merchant who pleaded with the princess for the ring, claiming that he had lost it there on another day. His long black beard and glittering eyes quite frightened the girl, who screamed for help and clutched the ring to her snow-white breast, while all her maids and ladies-in-waiting ran to her assistance. They surrounded their young mistress in a protective circle and then threw themselves at the dark intruder, tickling and pinching him so mercilessly that he almost went out of his mind. He laughed and cried at the same time, and screamed and howled and threw himself about, and sneezed, coughed, kicked his legs, waved his arms, rolled this way and that, threw himself flat on his face, and could do nothing to help himself because, unfortunately for him, he quite forget in all that excitement that he was a magician. It was only after a great struggle to come to his senses that he could change himself into a hedgehog from which the girls leaped away because they pricked their fingers on his spikes.

The princess showed the ring she had found to her father and liked it so much that she swore she'd wear it night and day. But next morning, when she was dancing alone in her room, the ring happened to slip off her finger. It struck the floor and changed at once into a young man who seemed so beautiful to her that she felt as if her eyes were burning. The princess became quite confused, and kept her eyes fixed on the floor with nothing to say. But when the sorcerer's apprentice told her his whole story she ran to her father and asked him to have the merchant thrown out of the gates if he came begging for his ring.

But that's not what happened. The black-bearded merchant showed up that very afternoon, cast a quick spell on the prince who ordered the ring returned to him at once, and the princess burst into angry tears. She threw the ring so hard on the ground that it shattered at the merchant's feet and turned into a hundred tiny pearls.

Immediately, the Greek shook and shuddered all over as if in some fever, fell flat on the floor, leaped up again as a large black rooster and began pecking at the scattered pearls. When he had gobbled up all but one which he didn't see, he flew to the window sill, flapped his wings and sang out: "Where are you now, apprentice?" Then he hopped high into the air and vanished.

One pearl, however, the largest, remained on the floor because the apprentice had taught the princess earlier what to do, and she deftly dropped her handkerchief to hide it from the rooster. It was this pearl that now rolled out from its hiding place, crowed "Here I am!" in a rooster's voice, and flew out of the window in a falcon's body. The falcon soon caught up with the chortling rooster, slashed its comb to ribbons, crumpled its right wing, then seized it with its talons, took it high into the clouds, and dropped it like a stone into a rushing river where it drowned at once. The brave bird flew back to his princess, perched on her shoulder and looked at her with his bright, shiny eyes, and then, when she laughed with pleasure, he hopped down to the floor and turned at once into the handsome young sorcerer's apprentice.

That was the last time that he practiced any kind of magic, except the kind that comes from love and goodness. He married the princess, brought his old mother to live in the castle, saw all his sisters married to rich merchants, and sent an order to all the taverns in the country that his father was to be free to drink whatever he wanted free of charge, for which the good son paid out of his own pocket once a year.

And soon after the death of his father-in-law, the brave and clever cobbler's son who had once been a poor sorcerer's apprentice, became an independent ruler in his own right. He lived a long time with his wife and their many children, and with such happiness, prosperity and peace for all his joyful subjects, that there is no way to record it with a pen, sing it in a ballad, or tell it with the tongue.

How a Smart Peasant Fooled a Stupid Devil

EVER SINCE DEVILS were thrown into hell, they've been crawling over this poor world of ours and bringing bad luck to people everywhere. They thought up every kind of crime and all the vices like pride, greed, cheating, hatred, spite, stuffing yourself with food, looking down at others, injustice, gossip, disobedience and disrespect for old age, from which came all the ills that give us all such a hard time today. There was never any hunger on earth until they got here, nor were there plagues, wars, poverty, despair, tears or complaints.

But all this happened far away at first, never in our land, where only honest country folk lived long, long ago. Everyone here tended the soil and worked for his bread, and the grateful earth paid with such abundance that one year's harvest was enough to feed the toiling folk and the people beyond the seas as well.

The Devils that lived in all the other countries heard about ours from merchants who traveled here, but they couldn't slip in among us for many, many years because our land was guarded by crosses, made of stone and iron, that stood on our borders. What they did, at last, was take the form of ducats brought in by the merchants, and that's how they started showing up among us, working for our misery and destruction. They didn't have it quite as easy in the past as they do today, because our people worked hard, took what God gave them and didn't ask for more than they needed, and though the Devils were smart enough among the foreigners, they lost their wits in the face of the old country ways. An honest peasant could turn the tables on them with so little trouble that the tricked Devil would clutch at his horns, gnaw on his own tail, and pound his head on the ground or against a stone. Later on, when the Germans started writing books, the Devils learned all kinds of fancy manners to confuse the people, and now our poor folks can scarcely breathe, they are squeezed so hard. But in the time when Old Nick was clever in the foreign ways, but stupid in ours, it was the other way around.

It happened, then, that there was once a good, hardworking man who could always spot a Devil, alone or in a crowd, no matter what that Devil made himself to be.

"If the Devil walks about looking like a man," he used to say, "look him in the eye. In a man's eye you'll just see yourself. But in a Devil's eyes you'll see a black pit, without any bottom, and that's how you'll know him. If he's hiding and invisible, take an egg laid on Christmas Eve and peer through a tavern door, or through any a knot-hole in a wall where they've got the shutters closed at midday, and you'll see the Devil at work in full form."

This good man always seized the Devil by the horns when he came to a tavern, sat on his neck and rode around the inn, and everyone thought he was just galloping about like a boy on a rake or a hobby-horse. Or he'd take him home, hitch him to a plow, and plow all his fields between dawn and sunset. At last, the Devil got so tired of looking like a fool, and his back hurt so much from pulling that plow, that he came to the peasant and asked for a pact at any price whatever. But the peasant didn't even want to talk to him.

The Devil scratched his head about that for a while, came around on another day, and offered a new deal.

"If you really want to get some work out of me," he said, "let me, at least, work because I want to, not because you've forced me. I'll do all the work you need done from planting to harvest, and then we'll share the profit."

"That suits me," said the peasant. "But let's also agree from the start how we'll do that sharing. We don't want to fight about it later on."

The Devil, pleased that he wouldn't be galloped around a tavern any more, or that his back wouldn't hurt for nothing, agreed to everything. "What are we going to share first?" he asked.

"We'll brew some beer," said the countryman, "and here's how we'll share it. People live on top of the earth and you Devils squirm in hell, which is down below. So the top of the barrel will be mine and you can have what's under. Now jump to it, bring some malt, hops, yeast, a pot and a barrel, and brew me the best beer that you've ever made."

The Devil brought everything they needed, got to work, and soon there was vat of good brown beer. The peasant poured off the liquid for himself and gave the Devil the yeast that lay on the bottom. Then the man stretched out comfortably, sipping his fresh beer, while the Devil tried to gulp down the chaff and the yeast.

"Tfui!" he cried. "It's bitter!"

"Don't worry about it," said the man. "You put in too many hops, that's all. Drink up. It's good for what ails you."

"Well, my belly's hurting like I'm going to burst!" the Devil complained.

"That's nothing," said the man. "It'll stop after a while so forget about it."

"That's easy for you to say," groaned the Devil and doubled up with pain, "but it's my belly that's rumbling like a haywagon on cobble stones."

"That shows you drank too fast," said the peasant. "You should take your time. But a good run behind the barn is the best thing for a bellyache, so get outside and start running as hard as you can."

The Devil groaned again, clutched his belly, and galloped outside, and he didn't show up again for about a week. When he did appear, he was so weak and shaken that he could hardly drag his tail through the door.

"Phew," he told the peasant. "If I wasn't as strong as the Devil, I wouldn't have lived through that beer drinking. You wouldn't believe how blown up I got, nor what happened later! Next time I'll take what's on the top and you can have the bottom."

"Good enough," the man said. "Go out and plow a field. We'll sow it, and what shows on top will be for you."

The Devil ran into a field, worked all night and finished by morning. The peasant planted turnips. When they were ripe, he took the sweet, juicy turnips for himself and gave the bitter leaves to the hungry Devil. It didn't take the Devil long to realize that he'd been duped again, and he insisted that from that day on he'd take the bottom share of anything they planted. He plowed the field again, and the peasant planted it with sweet-pea, and when the fresh green pods appeared above the soil, the man cut them, carted them to the bin, shucked them and had a tasty meal, while the Devil tore out the roots, shook off the dry soil, and started chewing on them as hard as he could.

Things went that way for a year or two and finally the Devil had enough. He wasn't getting anywhere with the clever peasant, who worked him just about to death, and whatever he got for his pains wasn't worth a thing. So he came up with an idea to make his life easier and maybe even give him a chance for the peasant's soul.

"See here, human being," he said to the man. "I don't want to be your partner anymore. It isn't good for you to spend so much time with me and I don't like the work. So let's make a different deal."

"Hmm," said the peasant. "I see that you like new things all the time. You don't like it when things are slow and steady. But I like the old way, and I'll keep making a fool of you like I've done before, unless you want to lend me a little money I happen to need."

"How much?" the Devil asked.

"Just enough to fill my hat," the peasant said.

"And when will you pay it back?"

"When all the branches on all the trees are bare."

The devil agreed. First, he thought, it wasn't long till autumn when leaves die and fall. And second, if the man wasn't able to pay what he owed, he'd have a good claim on the fellow's soul, and that would please his master, Lucifer, whose representative he was to begin with. With this in mind, the Devil ran to get his money, and the good countryman got ready to receive it.

He went to his smokehouse, under which there was a big stone cellar for keeping the foods fresh and the beer cool in the heat of summer, and he cut a hole in the trapdoor in the smokehouse floor. Then he knocked the crown out of an old hat and placed it over the hole.

The Devil came running back, poured one sack of gold into the hat, and then another, and another, and then a sixth and a tenth, and still the hat was empty because all the gold fell into the cellar. Amazed, he ran for more, and started carrying it in sacks the size of a haystack, until at last the cellar and the hat were full.

All this carrying and running wore him out. He mopped the sweat off his face with the end of his tail, managed a sick smile, and said: "I'll see you in the Fall?"

"When all the branches are bare," the peasant reminded. "That's the deal."

"Be well then," said the Devil.

"And you can go to hell for all that I care."

When autumn came so did the Devil, asking for his money. But the peasant took him to a stand of pine, and showed him the green branches, and the Devil had to go back empty-handed. The same thing happened the next year, and the next, because fresh pine fronds always replace the old ones, and evergreens are always green, as the name implies.

At last the Devil realized that he had been fooled. He rushed to the forest, worked night and day for several months, ripped all the needles off all the pines and firs, and came running to his debtor for either the money or the peasant's soul. But the man only took him to another forest and showed him more green pines than the Devil could count in a month of Sundays.

"We didn't bargain about this forest," said the desperate Devil. "The deal was the other!"

"You're lying, Devil," the peasant said calmly. "All branches means all branches, a deal is a deal, so go back to all the other Devils and don't come back until all the branches on all the trees are bare."

"But that'll never be!" cried the Devil. "So this is how I'm to lose my money?"

"Is it my fault that you're stupid?" asked the man. "You're the one that wanted a new pact between us."

"So how'll it be between us from now on?" the Devil was worried.

"The old way, if you like."

"And what about my money? How about if we make nine bets, and whoever wins the most gets all the money and your soul as well?"

"Agreed," said the man. "What'll we bet on first?"

"On which of us is stronger. Let's wrestle. Whoever gets thrown so hard that he can't get up again is going to be the loser."

"Suit yourself," said the peasant, "but how can you hope to beat me when you'd be unable to throw my old grandfather, who has to be a hundred or more, and who is sleeping right now in that cave?"

The peasant pointed to a bear's cave, the Devil gave a whoop and ran inside. He seized the bear by the throat with both hands, and the bear gave a frightful roar, crushed the Devil in its paws, swung him by the tail and started battering him against the rocks, and when, at last, the Devil came flying out of the cave, he couldn't get off the ground for three days.

"Well, I'm lucky I didn't take you on," he said when he came around again. "Your old grandfather is stronger than Lucifer, so what must you be like? But now let's see which of us is faster. You run and I'll chase you."

"Suit yourself," said the peasant. "But maybe you ought to try it first with my year-old son. There's no use wasting your legs against me if you can't catch a baby."

With this, the peasant pointed to a hare sleeping in a furrow, the Devil ran up to it and shouted "hoo-ha," the hare shot away like a bullet from a gun, and that's all they saw of it that day.

"Well, alright," said the Devil. "You've won that one too. And now let's see how far you can throw a stone."

He stooped, grunted, seized a massive boulder, and hurled it so far into the sky that the huge rock didn't fall to earth until an hour later.

The peasant had a lark in his pocket. He hid it in his hand, stooped and pretended to pick up a stone, and flung the bird into the air where it disappeared at once and didn't come down at all.

"So you've won that one too," the Devil admitted. "That's some arm you've got! But I bet I can carry that horse around the haystack quicker than you."

The Devil caught a carthorse, heaved him up on his shoulders, trotted around the haystack in about five minutes and stood once more before the peasant, panting and dripping with sweat.

"Oh you lazy slowpoke," the countryman said. "Here you grasp that horse in both arms, hoist him on your shoulders, put your back into it and pump both your legs, and it takes you five minutes to get around the haystack. I can do better with just my heels alone!"

With this the peasant jumped astride the horse, kicked it with his heels, and rode all the way around the stack five times in one minute.

"How did you manage that?" cried the amazed Devil. "But let's see who can squeeze more water from a stone."

He grasped a piece of granite in both hands and squeezed it so hard that a few drops of water dripped out of the rock, but the peasant only shrugged and said it was nothing. He bent once more as if to pick up a stone but, instead, took a fresh cottage cheese out of another pocket, squeezed it in one fist and the water ran from it in a stream.

"Well, you've won the fifth bet," the Devil conceded. "Now, who can shout the louder?"

He bellowed so loud that the earth trembled and a whirlwind swept across the field, but the peasant only went on twisting a wicker hoop about the size of the Devil's head.

"You'd better put this on," he said. "Because when I shout your horns will fall off, your ears will split in half, and your head will crack in four and fall apart, unless we bind it with this hoop, like a liquor barrel. And who knows if it'll hold even with the hoop."

"Don't shout, don't shout!" the Devil cried at once. "Why should I risk my head on a bet like that? I'll give you that sixth one. So now let's see who can whistle loudest."

The Devil blew such a shrill, ear-splitting whistle that leaves fell off the trees, birds tumbled out of branches, and dogs started howling in all the villages for ten miles around. But the peasant only shrugged and told the Devil to close his eyes tightly.

"Why should I?"

"Because when I whistle, your eyes will pop right out of your skull."

The Devil scrunched down his eyes although he kept them ajar just enough to see a little daylight, the peasant whipped a plaited rawhide thong from behind his back, and the rawhide whistled so hard and sharp across the Devil's eyeballs that he saw every star in the firmament, the comets and all. The earth seemed to spin under him, and all the air rushed out of his belly, so that he had to sit down to catch his breath.

"Shall I whistle again?" asked the peasant.

"No! That's enough! You win! But for the eighth bet I'll toss you over your own roof and then you try to beat it."

He grasped the man around the waist and hurled him so high into the air that the peasant flew across his own chimney.

"You're a strong Devil, I grant you that," the man said, somewhat out of breath. "But now it's my turn."

Night had come by then, there was a full moon riding in the sky, and the peasant squinted at it as he caught the Devil by the horns and tail and lifted him overhead.

"What are you waiting for?" the Devil demanded. "Get on with the bet."

"I'm just looking at the moon and my father who is sitting there. He's God's blacksmith and he wants to use you for a bellows. I'd like to help him out so I'll throw you up there as soon as he nods his head."

"You win! You win!" the Devil howled and started to tear himself out of the peasant's grasp. "The moon's too close to heaven and I don't want to go anywhere near it. You've won all the bets and the money's yours. And I won't claim your soul either, because that's our deal."

"That's not enough for me," the peasant said sternly. "I'd have been doomed to hellfire if you'd won, so I won't let you go till you promise that you won't bother decent working people anymore or lead them to temptation."

"You have my Devil's word on that," the demon assured him. "From now on I'll keep company only with the gentry."

"That suits me fine," said the peasant and set the Devil back upon the ground. "So where will you go now?"

"There's a princess I've wanted to torment for some time only I got so busy with you I forgot about it. Now I'll go after her."

"What's she done to you?"

"Nothing. She's a good girl, as the gentry goes. But she's been dreaming, she's become absent-minded and forgetful like she's in love or something. She moons about all day and forgets her prayers at night and in the morning. Such people don't only risk their souls but place their bodies in our power as well. This is too good a chance to miss and I'm going to get her."

"Well, even that's a good thing to know," the peasant shrugged and muttered. "And now, get out of here! I never want to see you in the countryside again."

The Devil took off at a run and the peasant walked home to his supper, pleased that he had got out of his debt so easily, and humming to himself. But in a few months the king announced throughout the land that his only daughter, who was the most beautiful princess in the world, was possessed by the Devil who tormented her each and every night. Whoever managed to drive out the demon would marry the princess and inherit the throne.

"I wonder if that's my old Devil," the countryman muttered, made a sign of the cross and set out for the capital, where the king gave him permission to try too cure his daughter.

"If you succeed," said the king, "then both she and the throne are yours. But if you fail you'll pay with your skin, because I'll have one strip ripped off your nose, and two from your back, and then I'll set my dogs on you."

The countryman wasn't a bit concerned. He put a lump of sharp cheddar cheese in one pocket, and a cake of lye soap in another. On top of the cheese he sprinkled some nuts, and iron musketballs on top of the soap. Then he got a bowl of honey and another of pitch and carried them at nightfall to the anteroom that lay just before the bedroom of the princess. There he set out everything on a table, lit a candle, sat down in a chair and waited.

At the last stroke of midnight an owl hooted suddenly, bats fluttered against the window panes, the double doors swung wide, and then the Devil ran into the room and stopped dead in his tracks.

"How are you, my old friend!" the peasant called out to the familiar demon and dipped his spoon in the bowl of honey. "What brings you here, eh? Maybe you've come to try our ninth bet?"

"No, no!" the Devil said hastily, glancing at the moon. "I'm here to torment the princess. But what's that tasty dish you're eating?"

"Honey," the peasant said. "The sweetest thing there is. Have some!"

And he pointed to the bowl of pitch.

The Devil seized a spoon and threw himself at the pitch bowl while the countryman went on eating honey and smacking his lips. He made it seem so tasty that the Devil couldn't understand why his own honey tasted like a tarpit. He kept glancing at the man and spooning the pitch into his mouth even though it made his mouth pucker and burned in his belly.

Then the man took a nut out of his pocket, cracked it in his teeth and enjoyed the kernel.

"What are you eating now?" the Devil demanded, still spitting pitch and squirming in his chair.

"Nuts," said the man and passed the Devil several musketballs.

The Devil rolled the iron balls around in his mouth, ground them between his teeth until his jaws were aching, but he couldn't bite through one of them.

"These nuts are too tough for me," he moaned, clutched his jaws and spat out the bullets along with some teeth. "I don't know how you crack them like you do. But I've got to leave you now anyway, I've got to start tormenting the princess."

"Let her be one night," the peasant suggested. "I've something really tasty for you here and you don't even have to crack it in your teeth. Just pop a chunk into your mouth and swallow it whole."

With this, the peasant broke off a piece of cheddar, threw it in his mouth, and smacked his lips with evident enjoyment. "Have some," he said, "and leave that girl alone tonight. She'll keep till tomorrow."

"No she won't," the Devil said, licked his mouth, and eyed the cake of soap that the peasant held out to him. "If I miss one night of tormenting that's the end of it. I'd have to keep at least thirty miles away from this castle."

"So eat some of this cheese to get your strength up," the peasant suggested. "It won't take you long."

The Devil seized the soap, threw it down his gullet in one gulp, and then he thought that he was back in hell but this time as a victim. His eyes bulged with nausea. A fire-breathing dragon seemed to leap to life in his swollen belly and twisted 'round and 'round, biting its own tail. His own tail started beating on the floor, as if to get away, and his horns shivered on his head with terror. At last he clutched his belly which had swollen bigger than a mountain, bent double in pain, and tried to take a slow, grunting step towards the door to the princess' chamber, but suddenly the morning roosters crowed and the night was over.

The Devil moaned horribly, his claws still clutching at his rumbling belly, and cast an anguished glance at the princess' door, but the countryman now stood guard before it while the morning rooster crowed a second time. One more cock's crow would put him out of business, the Devil knew, but now he had no choice.

He groaned once more and bolted from the room, just as the proverbs say it happens when a man eats soap, because that's just what he had done and the full effects weren't long in coming. In fact that's the way that saying got started.

From that time on the princess had no trouble. She got well. Her cheeks got pink again and her eyes got bright, and she could dance and sing all day as before, and two Sundays later the countryman became her husband and heir to the kingdom. Later, when he was the king and she was the queen and God blessed them with children, they and their people lived such untroubled lives that no man can describe it with a pen, nor in a song, nor even tell it fully in a tale.

As for the Devil, he was so disgusted with himself for getting the wool pulled over his eyes so often, that he went back overseas where his life was easier, and where he did so much mischief among the people, that Lucifer had to buy another hell to make room for their souls.

About the Ragged Prince and the Enchanted Horses

THERE WAS ONCE an unlucky king who couldn't raise a single child because each one died for one reason or another while still in their cradles. In the end only two sons remained. The older was strong and healthy and promised to grow into a mighty warrior, while the younger was small and frail and spent his time with books.

It happened one day that a sorcerer knocked on the castle gates, disguised as a beggar, and the king sent out alms, but the sorcerer demanded one of his sons instead. "Otherwise," he warned, "Death will carry off both of them as she did the others."

The Queen wept when she heard about this but agreed that the sorcerer should have one of the young princes. "We've already buried so many children," she said. "Are we to lose our last two sons as well? It's better to give up one if that'll save the other."

So the king gave up the frail, bookish boy and kept the young warrior, thinking that a warrior-prince would make a better ruler when he inherited the throne. The boy followed the beggar to a distant castle, which stood empty and unguarded in a magic forest, and the sorcerer left him there alone for a year.

"I'll be gone for twelve months," he said, "but you'll be alright here. Clutch at the corner of this table whenever you need something and it'll immediately appear. Make sure you sweep and clean this room every day but there are two rooms where you mustn't enter."

Then he gave the boy the keys to the castle and vanished into thin air. The boy spent the year reading and cleaning the room, as he had been told, and in twelve months the sorcerer returned just as he sat down to dinner.

"Well, how did it go here?" the magician asked.

101

"I liked it fine," the boy said. "I cleaned the room every day and I lack for nothing. Your table gives me everything I need."

"Good," the magician said. "I have to leave for another year. Don't forget to keep cleaning your room and make sure you never go into those other two chambers. Do you have enough books to read?"

"If I run out," said the youth, "I'll just grasp the corner of your table and they'll immediately appear."

The magician disappeared again, returned in twelve months, and the same thing happened all over again. This time the sorcerer said he'd be gone two years, and again warned the boy to stay out of the forbidden rooms, but two years were too long for the young man without anyone to talk to and he became bored.

"Why won't he let me go into those two other rooms?" he asked himself. "And what's the harm in seeing what he's got there?"

So he opened one of the forbidden rooms and found that it was stacked from floor to ceiling with books of ancient wisdom, among them one that told how to turn into any kind of animal or bird. There were more such books in the second room, and the boy sat down and read every one of them, but he forgot to do any of his cleaning. Instead, he searched the castle for more secret chambers, and found a great, deep cellar with an iron door, in which three horses stood in a pile of manure. There was so much of it that only the horses' heads were showing above it, and it would soon have covered them altogether if he hadn't found them.

The boy shoveled out the manure, and washed and cleaned the horses, and then he went out and found some oats for them, and brought them a bucket of fresh water.

"You've done us a great service, lad," said one of the horses. "That sorcerer is an evil man, who never forgives an injury or an insult, and he'd have roasted in hell a long time ago if he wasn't such a powerful magician. I was a famous prince, and these two were my brothers, but we refused to take him seriously so he chained us down here in the form of horses."

"We'd have been sure to suffocate in our own manure if you hadn't saved us," said one of his brothers, "so now it's our turn to do you a service. Get away from here as fast as you can because the sorcerer is sure to kill you as soon as he's back."

The boy left at once, remembered what he'd read in the ancient scrolls, and darted through the window in the form of a little falcon but the sorcerer went after him at once as a great black hawk. The falcon soared past a castle where a little princess was playing by an open window, and he flew into her room in the form of a dove. Then he turned into his own shape again and stood before her as a handsome young man. He told her of his danger and said that a cruel sorcerer would be shortly there, disguised as a beggar, but that there was a way in which she could help him.

"As soon as he's here I'll turn into a grain of barley," he said. "Throw it out to the chickens along with their feed. The old man will then turn into a rooster and start pecking at it and I'll jump onto your finger and turn into a ring. What happens after that will be up to you."

The little princess did just what he told her. She saw the old beggar turn into a rooster, then watched a grain of barley jump onto her finger and become a ring.

"He isn't here!" crowed the rooster after he had swallowed all the corn and barley she had thrown to him. "What's he turned into now?"

"Ugly monster!" the princess cried at him. "I wish the dogs would tear you into pieces!"

The ring leaped at once to the ground, turned into a wolfhound and tore the sorcerer apart, then the dog changed again into a beautiful young man. The princess wanted to keep him with her but he pretended that he had a long journey ahead, thanked her for her help, turned into a swallow and flew back to the three enchanted horses who were once more mired neck-deep in their stable. He shoveled out all the manure and watered the horses and they immediately turned into three tall princes.

"Now that you've killed the sorcerer," they said, "our spell is broken and we are free to leave but we will always come to help you if you need us."

They told him then to wash his hair in a magic tub he'd find in the garden, and each gave him a long horse-hair which they had worn in their tails as enchanted horses.

"Burn a bit of one of these horse-hairs whenever you need us," they said and left the sorcerer's castle to return to their own.

The young prince washed his hair in the magic tub just as they said he should and it immediately turned to gold. One of his hands also turned to gold, and gold dripped out of it instead of ordinary blood when he cut himself. But because he didn't want anyone to see his gold hand or his golden hair, he wrapped them both in kitchen rags and set out into the wide world disguised as a beggar.

His travels took many years so that he was quite grown when he came to the castle of a certain king and asked if there was anything he could do at court, but since he wouldn't take the rags off his hand and hair the only job they gave him was in the castle kitchens.

He worked there as a scullion, and he also helped out as a gardener's assistant in the castle gardens whenever the gardener had to be elsewhere, and one day the king's youngest daughter saw him through her window and asked who he was.

"Oh he's just the dimwit scullion in the kitchens," laughed the gardener. "They call him Raghead because he always wears those rags around his hair and on his right hand, and all he's ever good for is a joke."

"I wish I could see him just once as a handsome knight on a noble charger," Raghead heard her say, and the gardener laughed so hard he almost fell over.

Next day was a Sunday. The gardener had to drive the king to church because his coachman had sprained an ankle, having got drunk the night before and fallen down the stairs, and Raghead was left alone to act as a scarecrow and keep the birds from stealing all the buckwheat that had just been planted. The young man stretched in the shade by the garden wall and thought about the princess. He remembered what he heard her say, lit a small fire and burned a piece horse-hair he'd been given by the enchanted horses. A beautiful warhorse appeared at once before him, with a richly jeweled caparison and saddle, and with a full suit of costly armor and ornamented weapons piled on its back. He dressed in the silver armor, mounted the great warhorse and rode up and down the garden trampling the new buckwheat. Then the horse and armor disappeared and he lay down again.

But the king's daughter hadn't gone to church with her parents and her older sisters. She saw everything that happened. She didn't say anything to anyone about it but the gardener complained to the king about the ruined buckwheat.

"What's to be done with that Raghead?" asked the king and went out to look at the trampled garden, but the buckwheat grew taller there than it had before.

"What's the matter with you?" he shouted at the gardener. "Are you drunk or something? This garden has never looked better!"

The gardener hid for the rest of the day and abused Raghead for getting him in trouble. "You're just a no good lazy clown," he yelled. "A shabby vagabond, a disgrace and a laughing stock!"

But Raghead only said to him: "He who laughs lasts, laughs longest."

The same thing happened the next Sunday and the next, and the king finally lost patience with the irritating gardener and sent him to the kitchens to work as a scullion, while Raghead got the job of gardener in his place.

After a time the king sent word throughout the land that he wished to give his three daughters in marriage, and summoned all the greatest knights and princes to compete for their hand in the castle courtyard. He also had a golden apple made for each of his daughters which they were to give to their chosen bridegrooms. His two older daughters quickly made their choice, but the youngest walked all day among the ranks of nobles and didn't give her golden apple to any one of them.

The king was quite annoyed at this, because he wanted all three weddings to take place at the same time, so he sent out a second summons, this time to the merchants, artisans and craftsmen, and again several hundred young men stood waiting in the gardens for the princess' choice.

This time, when she refused to pick one for a bridegroom, the king became angry and told her she'd have to choose from among the servants. All the household servants were called at once, including the cooks, the grooms, the pot-washers, the gardener and the scullions, but Raghead wasn't there. They finally found him sleeping in the shade by the garden wall, and lined him up with the rest of the help, but the princess gave him her golden apple the moment she saw him.

Everyone roared with laughter. The two rich knights whom the king's older daughters picked on the first day laughed so hard that the whole castle shook. But all the princesses had now made their choice and a great wedding took place the next day. The king took the husbands of his older daughters to live with him and their wives in the royal castle, but Raghead and his bride were sent to the kennels.

It happened that soon afterwards the king went to war with a neighboring ruler, and his two noble sons-in-law were to command his army. It was agreed that the warring armies would fight three battles, one on each of three days, and whoever won the third battle would also win the war. Raghead begged to go as well but his brothers-in-law laughed so hard at this that even the king thought it was funny.

"Better you should stay home," he said, "and take care of my dogs."

But when Raghead went on pleading to be allowed to fight like a knight in armor, his brothers-in-law gave him an old, lame cart-horse that could hardly move and an old sword that was rusted solid in its scabbard.

"The war will be over by the time he gets to the battle field on that old nag," they assured the king, "and he won't embarrass us before the enemy."

Raghead climbed on the old, lame horse, and plodded behind the army. But once outside the city, he lit a small fire and burned another of his magic horse-hairs. A splendid charger appeared immediately as before, along with princely weapons and the finest armor, and Raghead galloped after the king's army. He wore a closed helmet so that nobody would know him. He could see from afar that the enemy was getting the upper hand, with the king's army in disorder and the king himself in danger of death or capture, so he charged bravely into the fight, steadied the king's army and turned defeat to victory. But he was wounded slightly in the hand, with golden blood dripping from his golden finger, and the king himself tore his handkerchief in half and gave it to the unknown knight to use as a bandage.

Everyone praised the strange knight who had come so bravely to their rescue and the king thanked him warmly for saving his army. But when he asked the stranger for his name, Raghead turned and disappeared among the other soldiers. The last glimpse that the king had of him that day was when he took off his helmet to mop the sweat off his brow when everyone saw his golden hair.

After the battle all the knights returned for a great banquet at the castle, and Raghead eventually got there as well, plodding on his old, lame horse and wearing his rusted sword. His brothers-in-law laughed and jeered at him, asking what great deeds he had done that day, and turning him into a public joke as if he were the court clown. But neither he nor his princess wife said anything about it. She merely found a chance to pin the scrap of handkerchief, with which her father dressed Raghead's wounded finger, to his table napkin. The king recognized it and wondered about it but didn't have time to look into it since he was getting ready for the next day's battle.

The same thing happened the next day. Raghead again won the battle for the king. But this time everyone saw his golden hand because his wound opened in the fighting and the king wrapped it up once more with one half of his own handkerchief. As before, Raghead's princess wife pinned the gold-stained bandage to her father's napkin at the victory banquet, and the king wondered how it had got there.

The third day was to decided the outcome of the entire war and Raghead proved himself even better than before. He rescued the king who was as good as captured, rallied the scattering army, and forced the enemy to save themselves in flight. Once more, the king sang his praises and, as a sign of special favor, gave his own signet ring to the unknown hero. But the strange

knight still didn't give his name and all that anybody knew about him was that he had a gold hand and bright golden hair.

This time Raghead asked his wife to place the ring in the king's wash-basin, so that he'd find it there as he got ready for the victory feast. She now had no doubts that her husband was the country's greatest hero. But while few other women would be able to keep their mouths shut about a thing like that, she knew how to keep silent and wait for what must surely happen.

The king was quite amazed to find his ring in his wash-basin, since he had given it to the unknown hero on the battle field, and asked both his noble sons-in-law to help him with an explanation. But all they could suggest was that an angel must have fought on their side so valiantly and given them their victory.

"Or maybe it was Raghead," they laughed again. "Let's call him. Let's ask him how he won the war on a lame cart horse and with a rusted sword."

The king agreed. "Was it you," he asked, "who pinned my handkerchief to my table napkin?"

"My wife did that," Raghead shrugged. "Not I."

Questioned about the second handkerchief and the ring, Raghead stuck to the same reply, and his brothers-in-law laughed so hard that the windows rang in the banquet hall. They led all the others in their jibes and jeers, poking fun at the patient Raghead, and turning him as before into a public joke, until he said at last:

"Sneer all you want. The proof is in the doing. Come out and fight me in the castle courtyard and we'll soon see who laughs the best and loudest."

The two great knights thought this was the funniest thing they had ever heard but when the king demanded an immediate contest they had to agree. Raghead excused himself, went quietly to the garden, and there he burned the last of his horse-hairs. An even finer battle charger appeared at once before him, carrying even more splendid weapons and armor. But this time there was no helmet that might disguise his face, nor was there a gauntlet for his golden hand, so that when Raghead rode into the courtyard everyone could see the famous gold hand and the golden hair.

His brothers-in-law had no more jokes to make. They knew they were in for the fight of their lives and charged him together. But he merely flashed his sword at them and their heads rolled off their shoulders on their own. Then the great hero who had once been Raghead told who he was and where he had come from, a prince's coronet was placed on his head, and he was proclaimed the heir to the kingdom.

The horse once again thanked him for the service he rendered to him and his brothers and was never seen again. But the new prince went on to become a mighty king, whose reputation as a warrior was so great throughout the world that no enemy would ever attack the kingdom.

About the Woodcutter, the Bear and the Rabbit

THERE ONCE WAS a woodcutter named Old Mike, a poor man who barely made his living, but he was a good man who believed in all the ancient virtues, and who trusted in goodness, decency and justice.

One day he went into the forest to split some kindling wood, when he heard a moan close by in the trees. It scared him, because it sounded like somebody was about to die and begging for mercy. But because he knew he had to help whoever was in trouble, he got his courage back again and went to have a look. What he saw was a huge pine that the wind blew down the night before, and under it lay a bear, and it was the trapped bear that was crying out and begging for pity.

"Have mercy on me, kind man," the bear pleaded. "Save my life. If I don't get out from under this tree I'll either starve to death or the wolves will get me."

Old Mike had a good heart. He was moved to pity. He set about rescuing the bear though it was hard going. First he stuck one pole under the fallen trunk, then levered another. He struggled as if his own life depended on saving the bear, and every time he got the huge tree lifted a little bit he pushed a new wedge under it. Sweat blinded him by the time he finished. All his bones were aching. But he saved the animal and went home.

Some time passed. Old Mike forgot about his act of kindness and went back to the forest to gather more kindling, and there was the bear that he saved before.

"Was it you who saved me?" the animal asked at once, and Old Mike nodded.

"Yes it was," he said. "And how are you doing?"

"Not so bad," said the bear. "Only I've got this gnawing pain in the belly,

111

like I didn't thank you for saving my life, so I've got to set that right straight away."

"What do you have in mind?" Old Mike asked simply. "I did what I did out of simple justice. I don't need rewards. You'd have done the same for me, I expect, if you got the chance."

"Would I?" the bear laughed. "I expect I would, one way or another. Only now I've got to pay my debt or that pain will never leave my belly. And because everybody in the world repays good with evil I'm going to eat you."

"Only bad people think like that," Old Mike shook his head. "There's still gratitude and justice in the world."

"How can you be so stupid?" the bear laughed so hard that he had to sit down or he'd have fallen over. "Still, if you find a judge who'll agree with you, I'll go along with that."

"I'll find one, don't worry," Old Mike said and went in search of someone who'd prove that living creatures still knew how to be fair. He met a peasant whom he asked to judge between him and the bear. The peasant listened to his story, nudged him with his elbow, and gave him a wink.

"How much will you give me?" he whispered in his ear. "I'll decide it any way you want, if the price is right. If it isn't, the bear will get you, because that's how it is with justice in the world."

"The one's bad and the other's bad," Old Mike scratched his head. "But I don't want the kind of justice you can buy or sell."

He went off to find another judge and came across an ox he brought to the bear, inviting him to decide the case.

"Do I look stupid to you?" the ox asked. "You'd kill me for a meal just as fast as that bear would do it. Why should I take one side or the other? I'll be happy if at least one of you goes to the Devil, and I don't care which! Hah! All I need is to strain myself giving justice to the likes of you!"

He bellowed, flicked his tail with contempt, and trotted away. Old Mike thought that his good heart would break. He thought that gratitude and justice were as common in the world as grass, created by God and practiced by all the creatures, and here a man, an ox and a bear had all proved him wrong. But he was sure he'd find a fair creature somewhere if he'd just keep on looking.

"What you need," a swallow chirped at him off a branch, "is someone who is neither too big nor too small. If you're big in this world, you eat, if you're small, you're eaten, so find a creature that's neither one nor the other and you might get justice."

"A sheep ought to be about the right size," Old Mike told himself and went to a sheep. But the sheep just stared at him with its mouth hanging open.

"What do I know about things like that?" it bleated at last. "I'm a sheep. D'you expect a sheep to have an idea? I just eat grass and go where my sheepdog moves me and I don't have to worry my head about anything. If you want a judge, go and see my sheepdog. He'll nip your tail, and bark in your ear, and he'll run you to where you have to go, and you can be a sheep like the rest of us."

When the bear heard that he grinned from ear to ear and then he licked his chops.

"My gratitude is killing me," he said to Old Mike. "It feels more and more like hunger, the way it twists and turns in my guts. So let's get on with it so that I can eat you."

"Wait!" Old Mike cried. "That's just a dumb sheep. No sheep has said or done anything worthwhile since God made the world, so why listen to it? Still, it put me in mind of the one good creature that knows all about loyalty, devotion, gratitude and justice."

Old Mike ran to a barnyard and got the farmer's dog whom he begged to decide the case according to the justice of the world.

"Justice?" the dog barked. "I'll give you simple justice! Last night a gang of bandits tried to kill my master. I warned him in time, saved his life and everything he owns, and today he kicked me so hard out of gratitude that I can hardly move."

Old Mike ran back into the forest and cursed himself for listening to the swallow. "What's size got to do with anything?" he asked. "Justice is justice, and it doesn't matter if you look down at it from the top or up from the bottom. I'll ask a horse! That's a good animal that works hard and carries his master and he's always ready to do him a service. He ought to know about what's right in the world."

The horse came when called, nodded once or twice, and said he knew about gratitude and justice very well.

"I do everything for my master," he said. "I carry him, I haul his wagons, I pull his plows and harrows, I even fertilize his land and make it rich for planting."

"And?" Old Mike was delighted.

"And for all that he starves me, and beats me with a whip, and cuts my sides with spurs until my blood and sweat flow for him together. Oh yes, I know all about gratitude and justice."

"Dear God!" Old Mike cried, bewildered. "Has all goodness gone out of your beautiful world?"

"It's people that taught animals about pain and suffering," the swallow chirped at once. "Look for your judge among creatures that keep away from man and live in the wild. If there's still any goodness in the world you'll find it in nature."

Old Mike found a fox and brought him to the bear and the fox said at once that he knew all about what was fair in nature.

"I can't believe you still haven't eaten this stupid man," he said to the bear. "What's the matter with you? You're big and hungry and gratitude has never filled anybody's belly, so what's fair about that? If you don't eat him straight away I'll have to rule that you're just as big a fool as he, and in all my years I've never seen one like him. Justice? Ha! I don't bother much about men and bears, but if he was a chicken I'd give him quick justice!"

The bear roared with laughter and rolled on the ground. "That's fair!" he gasped and wagged his paw at the despairing man. "Besides, you're getting thin with all that running after gratitude and justice, and I don't like to eat skin and bones."

The wolf came next, and his idea of justice was to share Old Mike with the bear, but the bear thought there wouldn't be enough gratitude on Old Mike's bones to fill both their stomachs.

"So that's that," said the bear. "You've had your search for justice. Now let's take care of that gratitude I owe you and get down to eating."

The sad woodcutter hung his head, and offered his soul to God, but he got the bear to agree on one more judge to decide the matter. He went off without a lot of hope but the swallow fluttered down at once and chirped in his ear.

"Who knows about right and wrong unless its a creature that does no harm to anyone but has to hide from everyone just to stay alive? Injustice is the best teacher. Find that kind of judge."

"But where can I find him?" poor Old Mike despaired.

"He's crouched down under a bush just a step from here. He's hiding from man, the fox, the wolf and the dog as well. Be sure you don't frighten him so he'll run away and you'll find out all about gratitude and justice."

The woodcuter found a rabbit and told him his story, and the rabbit thought he might be able to help. He went with Old Mike to the bear.

"Gratitude is hard to find," he told them both, "because that comes from living creatures, great and small, and so I've never found it anywhere. I know only creatures without kindness."

"Now there's a judge for you!" cried the bear. "He speaks from experience."

"But justice comes from God," the rabbit went on, "and it never misses anyone, as I'll show you if you take me to the place where all this trouble began."

They all went to the spot in the forest where the tree had fallen on the bear. The poles and wedges were still in place, holding up the trunk. The rabbit told the bear to crawl under the tree, so that he might see everything as it was and render fair judgment, and the bear squeezed himself under the trunk again.

"Now!" cried the rabbit to Old Mike. "Quick! Pull out the wedges!"

The woodcutter jerked the levers from under the tree, kicked away the wedges, and the trunk fell on the bear again and pinned him to the ground.

"Help!" groaned the bear. "This tree is going to crush me!"

"Now everything is exactly as it was," the rabit said. "Neither of you owes anything to the other. There is no gratitude to worry about and justice has just fallen."

Then he turned to Old Mike and sent him on his way.

"Go home," he said. "Give your thanks to God. Hurt no one. Try to be kind to everyone. Have gratitude and justice in your heart, which is where they belong, even if you're the only creature in the world who believes in them."

How the Princess Learned to Laugh

THERE WAS ONCE A PRINCESS who was unable to laugh. She couldn't even smile. She was the richest heiress in the kingdom, and as beautiful as the first day of spring, but she had no friends because no one likes a person who always looks as cold as a marble statue. Her parents worried about this for years, and the king, her father, made it known among all the people that whoever made his daughter laugh would become her husband. But since he also executed everyone who failed, to discourage all but the most inventive, few young men came to try.

It happened that another king, in a neighboring country, had two clever sons who believed that they'd succeed where the others failed because they were princes. They were strong, serious about themselves, confident and haughty, and thought that nothing was impossible for them, and he loved them both because they made him proud. He also had another son whom he thought a fool.

One day the oldest, who was the most clever, came to him and asked for his inheritance in advance so that he could make a proper showing at the neighboring court. He had no doubts that he would win the princess. The father didn't want to let his first-born go, but the confident young prince was so insistent that, at last, the old king relented, and his haughty heir set out the next day. He took food and money for the journey and also a jester's rattle with which, he thought, he'd make the princess laugh without any trouble. But on the way he met an old man sitting near a well and halted beside him to eat his midday meal.

"Spare a little bread for a hungry fellow traveler," the old man edged up to him and asked, but the proud prince shook his horsewhip at him and chased him away.

"Go to the Devil, you old goat!" he shouted. "Or I'll give you the biggest whipping of your life!"

He got to the city where the princess lived, and rattled his rattle, but the princess didn't crack a smile and, in due time, they rattled off his head.

His younger brother heard about this and decided to be more inventive. "I'll take a common rolling pin," he said, "because that's what the Lord of Misrule carries in the Fools' Day processions, and I'll appear before the princess like the King of Fools. I imagine she'll start laughing at once and that'll be that."

That's what he decided so that's what he did, taking along money for the journey and a satchel full of tasty roasts, fruits, breads, sausages and desserts. But, like his brother, he too came to the roadside well where the ragged old man was sitting, and the same thing happened there as before. The old beggar edged up to the eating prince and asked for just a taste of the bread, and the proud prince leaped up, enraged, and chased him away.

"Get away from me, you miserable old peasant!" he shouted and shook his rolling pin in the beggar's face. "Or you'll taste this instead! I'll give you such a crack on the head you'll see all the stars!"

Once he got to the capital of the neighboring country, the prince dressed up as comically as he could and capered like the King of Fools before the grim princess, but not even a flicker of a smile passed across her face, and soon his head was bouncing in the castle courtyard.

The bereaved father, who had lost his two favorite sons on a fool's errand, wept for many days. All that was left to him was a big, clumsy, silly-looking boy who didn't have an ounce of a prince's pride anywhere about him, and who'd been an embarrassment to him all his life.

"Do what you like!" he shouted at the lad who asked if he could try to make the princess laugh. "They can cut off your head anytime they want! And you'll get neither food nor money for the journey!"

The young man set out nonetheless, with only a dry crust that a kindly maid slipped into his satchel, and he too came across the old man sitting by the well where he stopped to rest.

"God help you, friend!" he called out as soon as he saw him and sat down beside him for the only meal that he had that day. As before, the old beggar edged up to him and asked to share his meal.

"You're welcome to whatever I have," the good-natured young man said with a foolish smile. "It's just a piece of old, dry bread, I'm sorry to say. But if your teeth are strong enough, eat hearty!"

So they gnawed on the crust together, side by side, and then the young man stretched out to rest by the roadside and fell fast asleep. He dreamed that the old beggar turned into a beautiful winged angel, who told him that he'd been sent to earth to see if there was still any kindness left among the people, and when he woke up he saw the most amazing coach waiting for him in the road. It was shaped like a pumpkin, made of solid gold, drawn by a golden goose and gander, and the coachman was a dog with crossed eyes and a golden nose.

The simple-minded prince got into the coach, the dog cracked a whip, and they soon rolled into the city where the princess lived. Everyone came to gawk and laugh at this strange conveyance, thinking that a circus must have come to town, but the foolish young man couldn't understand why they thought it funny. He pulled a golden nail out of the coach to buy himself some supper at an inn while the golden coach stood waiting in the courtyard.

It happened that the innkeeper's greedy wife was bathing in the bath-house and saw the golden coach gleaming through the window. She snuck out when everyone else was gone, as naked as God made her, and started scraping the gold with a kitchen knife, but once she started she found she couldn't stop. Some strange force glued the knife to the gold, and her hand to the knife, and there she was, still sawing at the coach, when the prince was done with his supper, got into the carriage, and drove to the castle.

Everyone laughed and gawked at the innkeeper's fat wife running as naked as a jaybird behind the pumpkin coach, and one of them was the local baker who quite forgot the bread baking in his ovens. When the bread started burning, he ran out with a baking paddle and started paddling the woman on her bare backside.

"I burned my bread because of you!" he shouted, but the same force that held her glued to the golden coach also held him behind her, and that's how they rolled to a bridge where an old laundress was washing clothes in the river.

She gaped at this amazing sight, and quite forgot about the clothes soaking in the water until the current swept them all away.

"I lost my laundry because of you!" she shouted, seized her cloth-paddle, ran after the baker, and started paddling him in turn. But the same force that held him and the innkeeper's wife running behind the carriage also held her there, and that's how they rolled into the castle courtyard.

The noise they made brought the entire court crowding out on the balcony, including the princess, and what they saw made them all double up with laughter. First came a golden coach shaped like a giant pumpkin, driven by a crosseyed dog with a golden nose and drawn by a golden goose and a golden gander, and with a good-natured, foolish-looking prince waving from inside. Then came a fat naked woman who sawed at the coach with a kitchen knife, a baker who paddled her bare behind with a baking paddle, and an old laundress who was paddling him.

"I burned my bread because of you!" yelled the redfaced baker. "I lost my clothes because of you!" screamed the angry laundress.

The courtiers lay gasping with laughter across the balcony rail and suddenly they heard a peal of silvery laughter they never heard before. They stared, amazed, and saw that the princess was laughing harder than anyone. Her cold, white marble features were alive with color. She laughed until tears trickled from her eyes. She laughed and laughed and couldn't stop laughing with delight at her ability to laugh, and the entire city started laughing with her.

They laughed all night and all of the next day, and the day after that she married the good-natured prince in the cathedral, and no one in the country was ever sad again.

So that's what happened. The simple-minded prince won through kindliness what his two brothers lost through haughtiness. He and his wife inherited her father's throne, while he succeeded his own father as king of his own country, and the two nations became one and prospered together. The golden coach, the goose, the gander and the crosseyed dog disappeared right after the wedding, and what happened to the innkeeper's wife, the baker and the laundress is another story.

The Changeling

THERE ONCE LIVED a couple, who were both getting along in years, and though they farmed well and made a lot of money they were often sad. What worried them was that they had no children and that a stranger would get their prosperous farm after they both died.

But then God gave them a fine boy, and they thought their worries were over, even though there's always something to trouble a parent. Three days after the christening the old woman had to run with her bucket to another cottage, to get hot coals for her cooking fire, but when she got back the baby didn't look right to her. She couldn't quite put her finger on it, but she just knew, deep inside, that this wasn't her boy but another baby. She thought its head was bigger, and its eyes had no color to them, and when her husband came home from the fields he thought the same thing.

"Only one thing could've happened," their relatives agreed. "A forest demon must've switched babies with you. She took yours and she left the changeling. You probably didn't scatter a ring of herbs around the cradle."

"Come to think of it," said old Uncle Albert, after whom the baby had been named, "I saw some woman running to the forest and clutching a baby at just about the time you went for the coals."

That settled it, and now there was real consternation in the house, because they not only had to raise a child that wasn't theirs, but one that was a changeling and not even human. Neighbors came with advice of all kinds. One old woman said they should beat the child, and beat it so hard that its shrieks would reach the forest, and the demon mother would run back to get it and bring the one she stole.

What else could they do? The old mother picked up the changeling, laid him across her shoulder, and smacked his behind, and the little creature howled so loud that its face turned blue, but no demon mother came with the real Albert.

In time, however, the old couple got used to the changeling and raised

121

him as their own, even though nobody could get really close to him because he wasn't quite like everybody else. His head was as big as a bucket, to begin with; he would never do what he was told, and eating was all he ever did well. He'd knock about the house all day, twiddling his thumbs and staring at the sky, and if someone said that something should be done, he'd lie down and sleep. Moreover, because people gossip about everything they don't understand, nobody wanted to have much to do with him and he had no friends.

Things went like that for years until the false Albert was about sixteen, and the old father finally lost his patience and told him to start earning his keep like any other peasant.

"Give a sign of life, you lazy good-for-nothing!" he shouted one day. "Get in the stable and chop some straw for the horses. Let me get at least that much use out of you!"

The changeling went to the stable, but chopping straw made him sneeze and itch, so he buried himself in the hay and fell fast asleep. The farmer found him there, whipped him with his belt, but the whipping didn't seem to hurt him. He took the beating without a whimper and left home soon after, telling his mother that he'd look for work with a kinder master.

The day he left was just after a terrible storm full of hail and lightning, when a cloudburst did a lot of damage, and many people said they'd seen cats and dogs falling from the sky. The boy was walking along a levee, wondering what else might have fallen with the hail and rain, when he saw two men who were carrying huge coils of rope and cable looped around their shoulders. Both were pitch black, as dark as chimney sweeps, and Albert thought that was what they were. But they were really storm demons, fallen from the sky when their cloud burst in that hurricane. They took one look at Albert and knew what he was so they invited him to come along with them.

"What will I have to do to earn my keep?" he asked.

"You'll find out," they said. "What have you got to lose? Do people treat you so well that you'd miss them? If you don't like it with us you can always leave, but you'll have a grand life and see a lot of the world."

Albert got some idea of what this was all about when they came to a cottage and asked for some milk, but it had to be milk from only a black cow. Then they came to a pond where a black cloud hung above the water, and when they snapped their fingers it came down to get them.

"Climb aboard!" they called out cheerfully to Albert. "Stretch out and take it easy. You'll get to see things people can't imagine."

At first the changeling wasn't all that sure that he wanted to ride on clouds with the two strange spirits, but then he shrugged and jumped on anyway.

"Up, Blackie!" one of them cried out, as if he was urging an old mare, and a great rumbling noise growled in the air around them. Up they went, high into the sky, and Albert noticed they were not alone. The cloud was full of demons, some young and some old. The two who brought him were the master craftsmen. Some of the others were journeyman storm demons and the rest were apprentices just learning the trade. Some of them caught clouds on ropes and herded them to where they had to go. Others blew cold air on rain clouds and made ice. Yet others chopped the ice into hail, or made snow, or rolled thunderbolts around from one place to another, or polished the lightning. They signed him on as an apprentice straight away and set him to work measuring hail in big bushel baskets.

Time passed, they flew over many countries and let the storms loose everywhere they went, and Alfred really came into his own. He learned to rope clouds and pull them about the sky. He made rain and ice. His masters liked him and trusted him with making all the snow for the coming winter. But one day they ordered the clouds steered back where he had come from, and when he drilled a hole in one of the stormclouds to peer at his home, he felt so homesick that jumped straight down and landed on the thatched roof of his father's house.

"Is that you up there?" his old mother shouted. "Isn't the farm big enough for you, so you have to climb a roof to sit on? Get down at once because there's a rainstorm coming out of that black cloud!"

"Rainstorms don't bother me," Albert shrugged, but he jumped off the roof and went in the house. There he stretched, yawned, and told the old couple that he'd been working too hard at the job he had, and that he'd come home to get a little sleep.

"What are you, a chimney sweep?" the mother demanded. "You're as black as sin! Go in the wash-house, you lazy layabout. You look like a Devil."

He went and washed but the water didn't make him look any whiter, then he sat down at the table, ate everything in the house, went into the stable and fell fast asleep. He stayed with the old couple after that but they still couldn't get him to do any farm work.

"I can do only what nobody else can do," he told them when they chided him about it, and after that they just shrugged him off and left him alone.

But he did jobs in and around the village that nobody knew about, and it was only later that they realized the services he rendered.

One day he saw a wind whirling in the fields, the kind that's called a Dust Devil, and though he shouted at it, it wouldn't go away. It whipped a cloud of dust off the country road and tossed it in the duckpond. Then it picked up all the sheaves of wheat that had been bound for stacking and scattered them across so many fields that nobody would be able to stack them for a week or more. The farmers who were working at the stacks cursed and prayed in turn but the Dust Devil just whistled at them and spoiled all their labor.

The changeling watched that for a while, then borrowed a knife from one of the workers. He blew on the blade, honed it on his heel, then took careful aim with one eye and sent the knife straight into the whirlwind.

The wind died at once.

"What did you do?" the peasants were amazed.

Albert shrugged and walked away, thinking no more about it, but the peasants couldn't get over it for days.

"He killed the wind," they whispered. "He stabbed the Dust Devil. That lad knows more than we give him credit for."

Gossip soon spread the story all across the county, and soon even the people in the town knew about the youth with the big head who could do strange things — so strange that not even hags, witches and Gypsy fortune-tellers knew anything about them. In no time at all people started coming to him, at night and in secret, for help with one evil spirit or another.

One day a troubled peasant came to him from another village and complained about a nightmare that was squeezing the life out of him.

"Every night it jumps on me," he wept, "and sucks all the air out of me. I don't know any more what to do about it. I've tried everything. I've locked myself in my room and padlocked the door. I've put a new knife under my pillow and an axe in my bolster but nothing does any good. I've gotten so thin that the next high wind is likely to grab me and carry me away. I don't know what'll happen to me if you don't get that nightmare to leave me alone."

"There's a way to do that," Albert told the peasant. "But I've got to sleep in your house as long as I'm needed and no one in the village can be told about it."

He went with the peasant to his hut, ate a good supper, and had a bundle of hay made up as a bed in a fireside corner. But though he left the door wide open all night long, and though a nightmare can slip through the smallest crack in a wall or window, it kept away this time and the peasant got a good night's sleep.

"If I could just sleep like that every night!" he cried, refreshed in the morning. "I'd be as right as rain! I believe that I need sleep more than I need eating."

"I'll see to that," Albert said, and the peasant thanked him with tears in his eyes.

Next day his hosts gave him a real banquet although there was only Albert and the two of them to eat it. The hopeful peasant and his grateful wife couldn't do enough for the young fellow who, just a year or two before, couldn't find a friend in his own village. They fed him scrambled eggs, noodles with milk, cheese, bread and fresh butter. The farmer's wife fried him a huge dumpling stuffed with fruits and cheeses. Her husband gave him vodka. He ate and drank better than he ever did before and slept all afternoon.

Then came the night. Once more the cottage doors were left open and Albert made his bed near the fireplace. Suddenly, something large jumped into the hut, hissing as it came. The changeling looked around and saw the nightmare in the form of a huge black cat whose green eyes shined in the murk like a pair of lanterns. The nightmare sat on the floor for a while, preening itself for the job ahead, then leaped on the bed where the peasant slept. Albert crept up on it, seized it by the neck, and started pounding it against a wall.

"Don't walk around at night," he shouted, "you lost, restless soul!"

Everyone was immediately awake but nobody dared to say a word. They just lay there praying that Albert would finally get rid of the nightmare, which screeched and wriggled and struggled and spat. No matter how it tried to get away, however, the youth kept a tight hold on it, carried it to the door and threw it outside, and only then did he shut the doors and bolt them from the inside.

"Is it gone?" the farmer whispered, hardly daring to breathe.

"For good," Albert said.

"But what if it was only an ordinary cat?"

But loud human groans came from the outside instead of a cat's wail and everybody knew that it had been the nightmare in person.

"From now on you'll sleep like a baby," Albert told the peasant. "That nightmare was made out of human spite but it won't ever torture you again.

Just take note of whatever woman limps around the village in the next few weeks and you'll know which of them sent that nightmare to you."

Then he asked for another meal, with bacon and potatoes on the side, ate a good breakfast and went home.

That's how the changeling became a local hero, ridding many other people of nightmares as the months went by, and then the squire himself came to call on him, asking for help with a troubling problem that had made life difficult for everyone for years.

What happened was that about a mile beyond the forest was a swamp near a road that many people used, where an evil spirit pestered passersby, pulling them into the bog along with their horses. The people even paid for a saint's statue to be raised in that spot but it didn't help. Whoever came that way, especially at night, was seized at once and dunked in the mire, and people said that a drowned man lived under that water.

This had been going on for years, maybe even centuries, and many travelers stopped coming to the county because almost everybody in that land had some experience with the drowned man's vengeance. One lost his horses and barely escaped alive. Another lost his horses and a wagon. A third got lost in the night, trying to circle that cursed spot by several miles, and wandered around with his wife till dawn. At last the squire himself, coming back from town where he'd gone to get some excitement, took the swamp road rather than go the long way around and saw the drowned man with his own two eyes.

"Get rid of him," he asked, "and you'll not only please God but the people too, because all of us have had enough of this evil spirit."

This time, however, Albert pointed out that not even the most useful service should be done for nothing.

"I've things to do at home," he said, "and I'm always hungry. A good workman, they say, is worthy of his hire, so if you want me to do what only I can do, you should give me something."

The people of the neighborhood took up a collection. Some gave wheat, some supplied potatoes. Those who could give money found a coin or two and said they'd give even more once the job was done. Albert took it all and gave it to his mother so that she'd never say again that he never helped.

Then, on the first night of the full moon he went to the swamp. He hid in the reeds and waited, but an hour didn't go by before the drowned man appeared.

"Things are bad," he muttered as he came walking straight out of the water, a cane in his hands. "People don't come by here anymore and I've nothing to do. Least I can do is have some fun with their hay."

He pranced across the fields where cut hay lay in rows to dry before bailing so that it wouldn't rot later in the stacks. Water ran in streams from the tails of his coat and soaked everything in sight. He even jumped up on the ready haystacks and soaked them as well. A thick, ragged mist rose from the sodden fields before he was done, and hung like a tattered cloak over the wet hay.

The changeling waited until the drowned man had amused himself enough and started walking back to the swamp, his cane in his fist, then he leaped out of the reeds, caught the apparition by the head and hurled it to the ground so hard that it bounced, while the earth uttered a deep, hollow groan.

"And who the Devil are you?" the drowned man howled, struggling up again. "Where'd you get such strength? I've drowned a lot of cattle in my time but I've never come across an ox like you."

"Well, now you've met your match," Albert whirled him in the air and bounced him off the ground again. "Tell me how you manage to live under water or I'll wring every drop out of you."

"But I can't tell you!" the drowned man groaned. "And I won't! What would I be worth if I told everybody the source of my magic? But I'll give you treasures beyond counting if you just let me go."

"Who needs your treasures?" Albert spat into his fists, knelt on the drowned man's chest, and started pounding him like a thresher. "How do you do it? Start talking or I'll shake the liver out of you!"

The drowned man struggled for a little longer. "Let me go! Help! What have I done to you?" But Albert wouldn't listen. He just went on shaking him and pounding all the wind and water out of him.

"Let's hear it!" he threatened, "or I'll knock the stuffing out of you, throw you across my shoulder, carry you to the village, and hand you over to all those poor peasants you've mired in your swamp all these years, and dunked in the water while you drowned their cattle!"

"Oh, alright, alright!" the drowned man groped for his cane and passed it to Albert. "That's what does it for me. It parts the waters everytime I want."

Albert forced the drowned man to take him home, deep under the lake, where the creature lived with his wife and daughters in a fine brick house. He had a huge fish dinner served to him at once and went home at daylight, parting the waters easily with the magic cane. Without that cane, the drowned man would never be able to leave the swamp again, so the river road would be safe hereafter.

"You live well," he said as he was leaving. "I'll be back for another fish supper on Friday."

The squire, the peasants and all the country thereabouts praised Albert to the skies when they heard the drowned man would never bother them again, and gave him the biggest breakfast he had ever eaten, but he wouldn't tell them how he brought that miracle about.

Not long afterwards a poor man came to beg his help. He was so poor that his clothes were darned and patched all over, and there were holes even in the patches.

"We have a really strange ghost in our hut," the poor fellow said. "It drags itself around all night, knocks everything over, and it chews up everything that isn't nailed down. I've never seen it but my woman says it's a thin, white shadow that squeals and groans and snaps its teeth at her. Maybe it's some lost soul doing penance there?"

Albert said he'd come by that evening. "Tell your wife to fix me a big supper," he ordered. But when he walked into the poor man's tumbled down, dilapidated hovel there was nothing set out for him on the table. In fact there wasn't even any table, just a board and trestles.

"My lord," wept the poor man's wife. "There's nothing to eat here. We're so poor I feed my children on wild herbs and berries."

"What? Not even bread?" Albert looked around and thought that he'd never seen such poverty anywhere. The place was little more than a shack, leaking everywhere, and the few odds and ends of furniture had come from a waste dump. "Well, at least light a fire in the fireplace. It's not much fun sitting in the dark."

"What'll I use for firewood?" wept the wretched woman. "There's nothing here except this old bench."

Albert sat down on the bench, feeling very bad about the misery around him, but the cracked old bench collapsed under him and he spent the night sitting on the cold, earth floor.

No sooner had the poor man and his wife gone to sleep in a corner, however, when Albert heard a strange squeaking sound. Then there was something that slithered on the floor as if a crippled beggar was dragging himself along, and then there was a clacking in the ceiling as if a hungry dog was snapping his teeth. He listened to all that for a while then got up and nodded.

"I know what that is," he told the poor couple. "You've gnawing poverty living with you here. That's a lot worse than drowned men or nightmares."

He went home without another word. The poor man and his wife thought that he was angry because he got no supper, and that they'd never set eyes on him again, but he was back that night with a honeycomb, cobbler's needle and thread, and a heavy mallet. When the impoverished couple and their children huddled to sleep in the corners on the bare floor, Albert took off one boot, smeared it inside with honey, covered himself with his coat and lay listening for that tell-tale squeaking in the cold, empty hearth.

Suddenly he saw something white and thin crawling out from under the hearth stone, then dragging itself in and out of all the empty pots, and peering into every nook and cranny in the hut. It scooped up every stray crumb it could find anywhere, and gnawed on anything that hadn't fallen apart, and it moaned, groaned, lamented and squealed all the time it did it, cracking its bony paws as if in despair. At last it came to Albert's boot and squeezed itself inside to get at the honey.

He leaped up, clenched his fist around the top of the boot, and quickly sewed it tight with the cobbler's thread. Then he took it and his mallet outside to see what would happen.

He sat on the poor man's doorstep in the light of the moon and listened as poverty squirmed and snuffled in his boot and then began to gnaw its way out with its little teeth. "No more of that!" he shouted, seized the mallet, and started pounding the boot and poverty inside it, and he battered it until he knocked all the teeth out of poverty's head, even though it wept and squealed and begged him to let things be.

Then he took poverty, still sewn up in the boot, to the home of the drowned man in the swamp. He had no trouble getting there. All he had to do was tap the water with the magic cane and it opened up at once, changing into a smooth dry road before him. But the drowned man's wife wasn't pleased to see him. Without his magic cane, her husband couldn't get out of the lake; he was bored out of his mind because he could no longer drown the animals, pull down the wagons and torment the people; so he turned her life into hell instead.

"That's alright," said Albert. "I've brought him a toy. He can drown it over and over any time he wants to. You can never kill poverty entirely, somebody is always going to be poor, but you can knock its teeth out, so at least it won't be gnawing anymore."

A few days later the same desperate peasant came running over to Albert's parents' home, but now he was neither desperate nor impoverished. His face was ruddy with new health. His eyes were clear and shining. He was beginning to put on some weight and his hands were steady. He invited Albert to his mended and comfortable home for dinner that night, seated him on a new bench behind a new table, and his wife served them the best and tastiest supper Albert ever had.

But just as charity ought to begin at home, so very often that's where trouble starts. Albert's old father came to him one day, complaining that he took care of everybody else but paid no attention to the family's troubles.

"I thought you'd take care of this yourself," he said. "But you seem to have time only for strangers. Ever since I got that fine field near the meadow, and my neighbor died, there've been strange lights dancing over it at night. It's as is somebody crept about there with a lantern, searching for something he'd lost, but as soon as you go near it, everything disappears."

"I didn't know about that," Albert said. "But I'll take a look."

He went that night with a bag of turnips on which he munched as he waited in his father's richest field, the one the old man got before he was born, and which he once shared with a former neighbor. It was a quiet night. Nothing moved anywhere near. But suddenly, at midnight, a strange man appeared out of nowhere, a lantern in hand, and started hopping among the furrows while muttering to himself.

"One man's gain is another's loss," he sang out over and over as he peered at the ground underfoot and muttered strange numbers. He wore a tight frock coat and a stovepipe hat, just like a small official, and he clutched scribbled papers under his other arm. Albert leaped up and tried to seize the apparition but his hands went right through the phantom's body and the spirit vanished.

This happened the next night as well, and also the next, and Albert decided not to try to catch or chase the ghost in the stovepipe hat but just to sit and wait until the spirit came to talk to him, which happened a few nights later.

"This field we sit in," said the ghost, "was stolen from your father's dead neighbor and I'm doomed to haunt it until that's put right. Your father had a suit with him, and bribed a judge to give him all these pastures, and the neighbor went and hanged himself. I have to haunt this land until it's back in the hands of his family, what's left of it now."

"Are you that wronged neighbor, then?" Albert asked.

"I wish I was!" howled the ghost, while flames shot out of his nose and smoke from his ears. "I'm the crooked judge!"

For once, the changeling didn't know what he ought to do. It was one thing to batter nightmares and hobgoblins, or to knock all the teeth out of gnawing poverty, but here was a lost soul doing penance in the place it sinned. Nor was his foster father much help when he talked to him about it.

"Ho, ho!" he laughed. "Is that what it's all about? It's more than twenty-five years now since I had that suit. I slipped that judge fifty roubles to rule in my favor, ha ha ha. That acreage is the best in the whole village!"

"So maybe we should give it back to that neighbor's children?" Alfred asked, but his father almost fell over in amazement.

"Are you mad?" he shouted. "Now I know you're not a real human! Save such advice for yourself, not an old man who's been around long enough to know the ways of the world."

Albert went away but he couldn't shake off the idea that wrongs should be righted. The best way, he thought, would be for him to marry the neighbor's orphaned daughter so that, eventually, all the lands would pass to his children, and the judge's ghost would rest in peace as well. But when he went to propose to her she only laughed at him.

"What? Me marry you? You've got a head like a bucket, people gossip about you, and you have a stomach nobody can fill. Your wife would have two cook your soup in one pot and your meat in another. Why, everybody knows you haven't done a day's work in your life. You snore all day and wander about at night like an evil spirit. Besides, they say you're not even human, but some kind of whelp of a forest demon. And I should stand before a priest with the likes of you?"

She mocked him and jeered at him so cruelly that he felt like crying. But what hurt him the most was that people called him a changeling, not a human being.

"I've got to go to that forest and find that spirit whose son I'm supposed to be," he told himself at last. "Let her tell me to my face whether she changed me for a real baby. And if she did I'll never come back here again."

He left the next day. Many years passed but he didn't return. At first some people in the village used to think about him but then everyone forgot, busy as they were with making a living. The storm Devils no longer drenched their fields with water because they knew the village had its own rain demon. The drowned man no longer bogged down their carts and horses, poverty no longer squealed in anybody's larder, and even nightmares gave them a wide berth, while the one that Albert had battered so badly turned into a good dream. Only the crooked judge hopped about the fields with his glowing lantern, and whenever Albert's father caught sight of him at night, he thought about his son.

"Where'd that do-nothing son of mine get to now?" he'd mutter. "Me and the old woman are getting old. Who am I going to leave the land to? Maybe I ought to give it back to that old neighbor of mine? Ah, no. It's best to wait. Something else might happen."

But nothing did for more than seven years, even though Albert's mother looked at her roof every day, because that's where she found him the last time he vanished.

And then one day people saw a strange, hooded man walking through the village. He was gaunt and worn. He wouldn't tell anybody who he was and he kept the hood drawn over his face. Dogs barked and snapped at him, as they did to strangers, but he didn't stop until he came to the house where Albert once lived. He knocked on the door, went in and blessed the Lord, and sat down at the supper table without another word. Only after he and the old couple were done with their dinner, did he explain himself.

"I'm Albert," he said. "But I'm the real one that the forest spirit took from you. The changeling is back with her, in the forest, and I'm home for good."

Ah, what a homecoming that was! People came running from all over the county to celebrate the return of the real Albert, and those who remembered the day he was stolen told so many stories that a hundred storytellers had enough to say for a hundred years.

About three weeks later Albert married the girl next door, the one who laughed so cruelly at the changeling, and the old couple gave them all their lands. It was the biggest wedding ever seen thereabouts, five musicians played, and everyone who'd ever known the changeling was there to eat and dance.

And it was only after they've celebrated for three days and nights that Albert rose and said:

"My dear friends, there's never been more than one Albert in this world. The forest demon never kidnapped him nor ever gave him back. There never was a changeling. What you had all these years was just empty gossip, and everything that followed was just a lot of tales that nobody would believe if they didn't want to."

But people would always rather gossip and listen to tall tales than to learn the truth, so they went on believing the story you've just heard.

How the Clever Servant Found the Haunted Treasure

THERE WAS ONCE a wealthy but tight-fisted lord living in Mazovia, who spent his whole life in amassing treasures, although he inherited great wealth and rich estates without shedding a drop of sweat to get them. Blinded by greed, not only did he never give anything to the poor, but he squeezed every grain of wheat and last copper penny out of his serfs and tenants, just like a vampire that sucks the life out of helpless people.

The unhappy people who worked on his lands were so worn out by work, misery and hunger, that they looked more like phantoms than good country people. But that only goaded the terrible old miser to oppress them more. They froze in winter in their rickety shacks, with half the roof gone and not even cold ashes in the hearth, but the greedy skinflint wouldn't let them have even the dead branches that lay in his forests. In spring, they foraged for acorns that they ground into flour for their only bread, and then died of bloating. In summer, they wasted away while working in the heat from sunrise to sunset, and in the autumn they drank themselves to death. Their cruel master didn't give them a penny for their work but paid them in script that they could spend only in his taverns. In vain did his kind, God-fearing wife plead with him to have mercy on his people. He only laughed at her, and shook his fist at her, and told her to keep her nose out of his affairs.

Greedy, heartless people don't trust anyone. They always suspect that everyone else is as cruel, ruthless and dishonest as they are themselves, so the rich miser who squeezed and cheated such vast treasures out of so many people for so many years, lived in fear that someone else might do that to him. He found an old stone tower crumbling in his forests and moved his whole hoard there in a single night, not letting anybody come close to him to help because he wanted to keep the place a secret.

The next day he fell ill. No one knows if this was God's way of warning

135

him to be a better man, or if he merely overtaxed himself while carrying his treasures, but he refused to call either a doctor or a priest.

"I'd have to pay them something," he muttered to his wife, and died cursing heaven and the earth and everything upon it.

He died cursing, unrepentant, and without confessing any of his sins, but because he was a noble, and the richest in Mazovia at that, the bishop allowed him buried in consecrated soil and he was laid to rest in the chapel crypt at the edge of town. But a few days later everyone could see that God's justice worked with or without a bishop, and that the suffering of the poor can never be ignored. That greedy soul, which practically drowned in wealth in the miser's lifetime, couldn't tear itself away from money even after death. The dead man rose from his tomb each midnight, stalked in his shrouds around the harvest bins, and vanished in the vast forest that spread behind his mansion, not to return to his crypt until the roosters crowed to announce the dawn.

A terrible fear gripped the countryside at first, and no one dared to stick his nose outside his hut from sunset to sunrise. Only dogs howled and wailed as the condemned soul made its nightly journey on the stroke of midnight. But, in time, the dreadful apparition caused no special comment. Even women and children grew used to it, and paid it no attention, and some of the braver lads even trailed behind it to see where it went. One night they followed it to a crumbling tower where it stayed until it was time for it to go back to its grave.

When this news spread to the tavern the next day, the old peasants who were drinking there guessed at once that this must be the place where the dead man sat counting his money. None of it had been found anywhere when he died, and his widow had little left to live on, but because she had been just as good to them as he had been evil, they went to her at once.

"If you'll send people to search that old tower, milady," they told her, "all of the evil that was done around here might turn to the good." But though her servants worked all day in and around that tower, taking it apart brick by brick until it lay in ruins, they came back empty-handed.

They tried again and again but each time the story was the same. They didn't come across even a clipped penny and eventually everyone gave up. But one shrewd lad, an indentured servant who worked as a hand in the mansion grounds, was harder to discourage. He thought up a plan to discover exactly where the treasures lay, and how to get them out, and asked the widowed lady to let him try again.

"God help you, Jan," she told him. "Do your best. If it's God's will that you find that treasure, and if I can make life a little easier for the people, I'll give you back your freedom and a share of what you find as well."

That Sunday evening, just before the sunset and the dark, wet night that the murky clouds had promised all day long, the stubborn young man went to the cemetery chapel with one of his brothers. He was the best-liked fellow in the village, always as ready for hard work as he was for play, and he wouldn't take any back talk even from the Devil. He and his brother broke open the oak chapel doors, unlocked the heavy iron grating in front of the crypt, and the brave lad prepared to descend into the vault where the dead were buried. He lit a pine torch, crossed himself three times and marched down the stairs, while his brother locked all the gates and doors behind him and went home, sworn to tell nobody about this.

Once in the vault, the shrewd young man soon spotted the tomb of his former master, along with a fresh pine coffin that was propped beside it. It happened that a beggar had died the same day but the sexton was too lazy to dig him a grave, and so the beggar's body was put here for storage until gravediggers could be hired on Monday. Jan set the new coffin down on the stone floor, pried out all the nails and then pulled out the corpse. He hid the dead beggar in a dark corner, wrapped himself in his winding sheet and climbed into his coffin, and then he drew the lid down on himself and waited for midnight.

At the first stroke of midnight a terrible groaning sounded from the miser's tomb, the stone slab on top of it fell back with a dreadful crash, and the dead man rose. He was all grey and green, and a scarlet light burned like the flames of hell in his staring eyes, while his teeth clattered in his skull like a hungry dog's. That hellish light was so bright that it lit up the crypt, darkened all the shadows, and trembled among the cobwebs like a living fire.

Jan watched him through a crack in his own coffin lid and started shaking from his toes to the cowlick on top of his head, while the rest of his hair stood straight up in the air. He was a brave, devil-may-care fellow but this was just too much. Still, he had a job to do, the fear would keep for later, and he threw back the lid of his coffin and climbed out as well.

"Who are you?" groaned his dead master.

"Your servant Jan, my lord," he said, "here to serve you after death as I did in life."

"So you're dead too, are you?" asked the ghost.

"As dead as a door nail, sir," the young man assured him. "I couldn't live after you died, my lord, so I starved myself out of sheer grief and begged with my dying words to be buried with you."

The phantom, as distrustful in death as he had been in life, walked all around the lad, sniffing in suspicion, but he didn't catch the scent of a living soul, because the beggar's shroud that Jan had wrapped around him smelled not only of the dead but of rank poverty as well.

"When did you die, then?" the phantom demanded.

"Saturday night, m'lord," Jan said. "Got buried this morning."

"Are you in heaven or in hell?" asked the ghost.

"I go where you go, sir," Jan said. "Up or down, it makes no difference to me. I won't leave your side even for a moment."

The dead lord pondered this for a while, then nodded and told Jan to get a torch and light his way upstairs, but the shrewd lad didn't want a specter behind his back.

"It's not right, sir," he said, "that I should walk before you even after death. You go first, m'lord, and I'll follow you like I did when we were both alive."

The phantom shrugged and walked slowly up the stairs, and the lad followed, wrapped in his own shroud and groaning like a ghost. When they came to the huge, locked iron grating, the apparition ordered it to open and it sprung wide at once. The same thing happened with the thick oak doors that Jan's brother had padlocked behind him. The dead man simply shouted "Open before me, doors!" and then "Lock behind me!" and that's all they needed.

It was even more frightening in the cemetery where Jan saw whole companies of spirits rising from their graves everywhere around him. Some knelt to pray in front of their own crosses. Others sat on their tombstones, sobbing and groaning sadly, while all kinds of ghouls, banshees and vampires hopped across the cemetery wall and ran to the village to suck the blood out of sleeping people.

The doomed soul of his greedy master led Jan to the orchards behind the mansion, and then into the forest and the ruined tower, and there it stopped before a huge millstone that lay half-buried in the rubble on the tower floor. A tree grew out of the hole in the middle of it, and thick roots anchored it to the ground beside it, and no one thought there could be anything under it when they searched the tower.

"Open before me, door!" the phantom demanded and the millstone stood on end and rolled away along with the tree, showing a deep dark hole as steep as a well, with rotted narrow stairs leading into it. Down these steps they went, the phantom leading and the servant following, until they came to a vaulted cavern that shined with a red light like the phantom's eyes. Huge jars and cauldrons, filled with gold and silver, glowed in that evil light all along the walls, and bags and barrels of small coins, squeezed out of the peasants, stood stacked on top of each other all over the floor.

The phantom counted his hoard all night long, beginning with the last coin he amassed while he was alive and ending with the first, and just before first light he and Jan started back to the cemetery.

"Doors! Lock behind me!" Jan cried, walking behind the phantom, but the toppled millstone stayed just where it lay because the words of a living man had no effect on it. The same thing happened with the oak chapel doors and the iron grating of the crypt, although Jan made it sound as if he had locked them. He and the dead man were back in their coffins just at the moment when the crowing roosters sent out their first call in the village, and the miser's tomb closed on him with a crash.

But Jan leaped out of the beggar's coffin in a flash. He ran outside, cut and sharpened a stake of aspen wood, plaited a long rope out of willow branches, and went back into the crypt again. There he pushed back the stone lid of his master's tomb, drove the aspen stake into his dead heart, and bound the lid back in place with nine lengths of willow, so that the phantom would never walk again.

Back in the chapel, he offered thanks to God, and ran to the kind widow of his cruel master, whom he told everything that happened. She had four wagons, each drawn by four horses, sent with him to the tower, and by nightfall all the treasure was in her hands again.

Next Sunday, when all the poor village people came to church to beg for God's mercy, she had Jan bring the treasure to them and divide it in a way they had both decided. One quarter went to the church and for the masses to be said for the rest of all the troubled souls that wept in the churchyard. One was shared evenly among all the people whom the dead man robbed, hurt or cheated throughout his whole life. One quarter went to the widow and the last to Jan.

And so the brave, clever and hard-working lad who started life as an indentured servant to a cruel master, became a rich landowner in his own right, but he went on living in a simple house and keeping simple ways. His tenants sing his praises because he treats them fairly, and he feeds any hungry beggar who knocks on his doors.

He is still up there, living in Mazovia, and welcomes any traveler to his dinner table, so if you doubt the truth of what you've just heard, you can go there and hear it from the man himself.

The Woodcutter and the Devil

THERE ONCE LIVED an honest, pious and hardworking woodcutter who was very poor. He had an ailing wife and four little children in his shabby cottage, and he could barely feed them, having almost no time to till his patch of land, since he had to work four days a week for the master of the manor.

Then, as if this were not enough for misery, God saw fit to inflict a long and terrible illness on his wife. Trying to do all he could to save her, the poor man stripped himself of everything he owned, so that soon all he had left within his four bare walls was a cold stove, a rickety bed, and the mortar in which he ground and pounded grain for the wheatcakes on which he fed his family. But once he'd sold off everything else he had, and turned his grain sacks inside out in search of some stray kernel, he found that he didn't even have a cupful to grind.

His wife lay groaning on a straw pallet, too weak to lift a hand; his hungry children were crying for a crust of bread; and the wretched man knew that he'd come at last to the end of his rope. Nothing was left for him but to beg for help from his master whom he avoided like the plague when he had the choice.

Oh, what a master that was! People said he had a heart of stone, but that would make stones as soft and warm as butter on a stovetop. He started out as an indentured servant, became a manor foreman and the village headman, and then tricked and connived his way into the confidence of an ailing master, whom he robbed and cheated until he had to borrow money from his own sly servant. When this good master died, having signed over most of the estate to his plotting foreman as pledges for the loans, the jumped-up peasant threw the widow out of the manorhouse, and started his own rule.

The truth of it was that he did quite well, squeezing the last grain of corn and the last piece of timber out of his estate, but he also choked the last ounce of strength and the last copper penny out of his poor people. There was a

141

saying in the county that he'd tear the bark off the trees and the skin off the people if he could think of a market for them.

Whatever kindness there was in the peasants' lives before this former peasant became their lord and master went out of the window. There wasn't a shred of goodness or piety about him. If someone greeted him with the customary "Blessed be the Lord," he'd never answer "For ever and ever, amen," as decent folks do. When rain or sunshine came at a wrong time — that is to say a time that was inconvenient for him — he cursed so horribly at everything that was holy that people found their hair standing bolt upright on their heads with terror. If a beggar ever came knocking on his door he'd never give him anything; instead, he'd jeer at him, and play tricks on him, and laugh in his face. And since he had the habit of shouting "Devil take it" whenever he was angry about something, the people whispered that the Devil might do just that sometime, and that was the only comfort they had in their misery.

No wonder then, that the poor woodcutter thought long and hard before he went for help to this crude, cruel, spiteful, unforgiving and greedy exploiter, who took such pleasure in his tyrannies. But what else could he do? So he took his courage in both hands, bowed to the ground before this heartless man, and begged him for some food for his starving family, swearing on his soul that he'd either replace every bit of it, or work it off after the harvest in his own scant time.

He should have saved his breath. The master didn't even listen to the end of his pleading.

"And if that lazy woman of yours keeps lying around all day," he shouted, "pretending to be sick instead of going out to work in the fields, I'll have you all thrown out of that shack of yours and you can beg on the highways, for all that I care!"

Quite broken and without any hope of finding even a crust of bread for his wife and children, the poor woodcutter asked help from his neighbors. But it had been a lean year for everyone, everything cost too much, and everyone had barely enough for his own family and himself. All the poor man could get was a single handful of corn, enough for one biscuit, but he thanked God for that much anyway. He ground the corn into flour as soon as he got home, baked it into a cake, and divided it between his wife and children.

He didn't eat anything himself so that his children might get the extra crumbs. But he scraped the chaff and corn dust from the sides and bottom of the mortar and baked himself a biscuit out of that. With this in his pocket, he dragged himself to work in his master's forest.

That day he happened to be working near a murky swamp where, as the people said it, a Devil was living. But sick with worry as he was, and busy with his work, the poor man didn't even think about such stories. He stripped down to his shirtsleeves and started cutting down a tree that his master wanted hauled to a lumber mill.

The sound of the axe biting into timber brought a curious Devil running from his lair. He saw a woodcutter toiling at his labor. He also knew at once that the man was desperately poor, that he had eaten nothing since the day before, and that he had only a solitary corncake in his pocket. Since human misery makes a Devil happy, he crept up to the man's discarded coat, picked the corncake out of his pocket and tossed it into the bubbling black swamp behind him. Then, pleased with his own malice, he ran to hell as fast as he could to boast about how cruel he had been.

But there his pleasure ended very quickly. The senior Devil may have been a demon but he had more of a conscience and a better heart than many people who walk the earth pretending to be Christians.

"You went that far?" he roared. "You dared, you miserable bungler, to give such a bad name to us all? And what's the point of stealing the last piece of bread from a decent man who never did anyone any harm, who worked hard and honestly all his life, and who'll go straight to heaven the moment he dies? Get back there at once, you mindless ox, and keep that man alive! Work your horns off for him as long as he wants you! And don't ever bring such disrepute to Devils again!"

The swamp Devil tucked his tail between his legs, flew out of hell as if all the bats were after him, changed his horns for a peasant's cap and landed in the spot where he left the man. Worn out with work and wondering what happened to his corncake, the poor woodcutter was sitting under a tree in complete despair. He hung his head quietly on his chest and two large tears rolled down into his beard. There was something so terrible in the silent suffering of that poor, good man, and in the absolute end of all his hope, that even the Devil shook with shame at his stupid trick.

"Why all the tears, brother?" he asked, stepping up.

"What else have I left?" The wretched man was ready to end his own life but he could not leave his sick wife alone in the world nor orphan his children. "It's two days since I've had food in my mouth. I'm too weak to work. And now some Godless creature stole the last crumb I had. Who could be so low? It must be that Devil that lives in this swamp. No human being would pull such a trick."

"Huh!" the Devil muttered, not daring to look him in the eye. "The Devil's not as black as he's painted. But how come you let such terrible poverty get its claws on you? Maybe you whooped it up a little too much and are paying for it?"

"What else but poverty could come from such a life as mine?" the woodcutter groaned. "I work four days a week, from sunrise to sunset, for the lord of the manor, and for that I get a one-room hut that's falling around my ears and the use of a patch of land the size of a bedsheet. Whatever time I've left hardly pays for a pinch of salt. And now my woman's sick, in bed for eight weeks already and not getting better. The last thing I had in the house I sold today. The only thing left for me is to watch the death of my children."

His eyes filled with new tears and he let his head hang brokenly as before.

"Wait a bit, neighbor, wait a moment there," the Devil said, helped him to his feet, and slipped his arm familiarly inside the man's elbow. "Everything will go well for both of us, take my word on it. Use me as your helper, and when you've a job to do for your master I'll earn enough to feed all of us. I was just looking for a job somewhere, but you know how tough it is to find work this time of the year. Just give me a corner of your hut to sleep in and let me get to work. Believe me, I can work as hard as the Devil if I want to."

"It's your choice, my friend," the woodcutter sighed. "I've never denied a place to sleep to any poor soul, you can have your corner, but I've got to warn you we've got nothing but poverty at home. You'll have a hungry start with me, I'm sorry to say."

"Not as hungry as you think," the Devil said, took bacon, bread and a jug of vodka out of his traveling bag and shared it at once. "By the way, I heard somewhere along the way that your master wants to turn all this timberland into grazing land. Go make a deal with him right away and we'll clear this forest."

"How can we do that?" the woodcutter sighed. "There's more than 200 acres here. It'd take us years. And the master wants it all done straightaway."

"I'll think of something," the new helper said, "don't worry about it. You just go right up to the manor and make your deal today."

The woodcutter found the Devil's confidence very strange indeed. But, as he asked himself, what did he have to lose? And why should another honest workman get him into trouble? He took his helper at his word, went to see the master, and made a deal to cut down the forest for 1,000 crowns and a hundredweight of wheat.

That night, as soon as dusk had fallen, the woodcutter's helper brought bread, cheese and a roast for his new master's family, and got ready to start chopping down the forest. He tried to talk him into staying home with his wife and children but that honest man wouldn't hear of letting him do all the work alone. He took his axe and went to work as well. But when they got to the clearing he saw that his strange new helper hadn't brought an axe of his own.

"You'd better go back and get it," he sighed as he got set for work, but the Devil only laughed at him.

"That's the trouble with people," he said, grinning from ear to ear. "We'd never get all this timber down with ordinary tools even if you had ten men working for a year. So just you sit down here, master, and I'll show you what kind of help I've called up for us."

With this the Devil strode deep into the forest and a frightful wind sprung up there at once, howling among the trees like a flock of demons. Tall pines, huge oaks, chestnut trees and maples whirled up to the sky and fell back to earth with a noise like thunder. Thick roots were ripped right out of the soil. Stumps flew about like kingpins.

Scared half out of his wits by this infernal show, the woodcutter ran out of the forest and stood bewildered in the fields, waiting for his helper. But when the poor fellow didn't come back in more than an hour, and the terrible destruction showed no sign of ending, he said a prayer for his helper's soul and went sadly home.

The Devil didn't get back to the cottage until dawn, and the poor woodcutter greeted him with joy. He thought his friend was dead, crushed by one or another of the falling trees, and here he was back after a whole night's work and asking him to come out and see what he'd done.

Curious to see what anyone could do in such a dreadful storm, the woodcutter went with the Devil back to the forest and stood struck dumb with amazement when he looked around. All of the trees were down, roots and all. Not a twig was upright. The whole vast acreage for which he contracted with his master was as flat as a potato pancake. Moreover, all the logs had been cut, trimmed and stacked and ready for the market.

"How did you do that?" he gasped, unable to believe what his eyes were seeing.

"I told you I've a way," the Devil said with a modest smile. "All that's left is to call your master, show him what we've done, and to collect our wages."

The words were no sooner out of his mouth when they heard hoofbeats clattering behind them and saw the former peasant, now puffed up like a magnate, riding with his dogs. The hounds threw one look at the woodcutter's new helper, howled in terror and fled with their tales between their legs, and the poor man got suddenly very worried. He'd already started to get a bit suspicious about whom he was dealing with, but at this sight he turned numb all over.

Edging a little away from the Devil he started whispering prayers to the Holy Mother, but the landlord who believed in neither God nor Devil, saw only the profits he would make out of all this pasture, the cordwood, and the crops he'd have planted there. The price he promised to pay for all this work was nothing in comparison.

"Not bad," he said, surprised to see so much done in a single night. But the woodcutter was too honest to take all the credit.

"My helper did it all, my lord," he said. "He should get all the money."

"No, no!" the Devil cried. "Ai, what are you saying, master? I agreed to work for you for a place to sleep and for a warm corner by the fireside. What I earn is yours!"

"Do what you like about that," the landlord shrugged since he meant to cheat his workers anyway. "But one of you had better come with me to the manor to collect the money. Maybe I'll find something else for you to do."

With this he turned his horse around and walked it away and the Devil followed him a few minutes later. He took his time, letting the greedy landlord do what he knew he'd do, and in the meantime the fellow was rubbing his hands with glee. He had been ready to pay twice as much for having the woods cleared. He quickly found 1,000 crowns' worth of coins of one kind or another and then thought he'd squeeze a little more out of two trusting peasants.

"They'll never know the difference," he grinned in contempt, "if I switch ten gold crowns for ten silver thalers. And if they do, they'll be afraid to say anything."

He'd no sooner done that when the woodcutter's helper came knocking on his door.

"Well, peasant, here you are," the great lord said grandly. "Here's a thousand for you. That's a nice bit of money you've earned for yourself, there

146

aren't many who'd give you as much for what you did. Count it well, so you won't say later that I tried to cheat you."

But the helper bowed humbly and said he put his trust in the great lord's honesty and conscience, which is exactly what a real peasant would say to his master, took the money without counting it and left. He heard the landlord laughing almost all the way to the woodcutter's hut.

"My friend," the woodcutter said to him in a nervous voice. "You know I didn't earn this. You did all the work. So take the money and go."

"What's wrong," cried the Devil. "Why do you want to get rid of me? What have I done? Did I lead you astray or drive you to despair? Hey, it's not right to kick out a man after you've invited him into your house."

"That's true enough," the woodcutter scratched his head, embarrassed to show such poor hospitality even to a helper. "You don't really need my corner now that you've so much money, and anyway, to tell you the whole truth, there's something funny about the way you work. It seems to me that you've either palled up with a Devil, or that you're one yourself."

"Haw haw!" roared the Devil. "You've some sharp wits in your head, my friend! But what if I am one? I'm not asking for your soul. I'm not even leading you to sin. All I want is that you take this money which you've earned one way or another for years. Think of it as payment for that corncake I stole yesterday. If you don't take it, I've got to stay with you until my debt is paid, and who wants a Devil at his heels for ever? Besides, it's real money, it's not Devil's magic. Ask your priest tomorrow if it's safe to keep it."

The Devil's logic made sense to the woodcutter who took the money and hid it under his wife's pillow.

"But," said the Devil, getting up to leave, "your landlord cheated you with ten silver thalers. Let me collect on that and we'll be quits."

"Gladly!" the woodcutter cried. "Keep whatever you get out of him, and let this be the last that I see of you."

Shaking hands, they parted as the best of friends, but each knew it was better they never met again.

It happened that night that the master was sitting in his manor, toasting his boots at the fireplace, smoking a long-stemmed pipe and sipping his tea, when the doors opened and the Devil walked in, still in his role as the woodsman's helper.

"What do you want?" the landlord barked in his usual manner.

"Begging your lordship humbly," the Devil murmured, bowing to the ground. "I've come about that payment. We found ten silver thalers instead of ten gold crowns when we counted it. I know it didn't happen on purpose, my lord... a great lord like you, sir, doesn't cheat the people... but anybody can make a mistake..."

"What?" roared the man, puffing clouds of smoke. "I counted every dime a dozen times over! Every penny's there! You think you can wheedle more out of me, your dumb peasant scoundrel?"

"Oh no sir, no sir," the Devil wailed, playing the frightened peasant. "May the Devil take me if that's what I wanted!"

"And may the Devil take me if I cheated you out of a penny!" the man roared again and leaped to his feet to throw the intruder out of his house.

But those were the words for which the Devil waited. In one flash of fire and one puff of brimstone, the humble peasant turned into his real form, complete with cloven hooves, great horns like a ram and a long, black tail. He seized the howling landlord by the neck, tore the soul out of him, clutched it in his claws, bounded with it right out of the chimney and took it straight to hell.

The man's lackeys found him a little later when they came to clean up after him and put him to bed. A doctor came from town and couldn't revive him. He scratched his head and cleared his throat a lot, but all he said was that the master of the manor must have had a fit.

Next morning the woodcutter found a priest and made a confession. Since he set out to earn the money in good faith and the work was done, it was no sin for him to keep it, his confessor told him, and he not only had enough to feed his family in bad times from that moment on, but also to help his good woman back to health again.

As for his Devil helper, he became such a hero among the other Devils for the way he tricked the bad lord of the manor and carried off his soul, that he was made Chief Devil in charge of collections, moved to hell, and was never seen near the swamp again.

Escape from the Witch

PEOPLE SAY that once a witch has you in her power, and keeps you imprisoned under an evil spell, there is no way to get away from her but that isn't true. There are good spells as well as black magic, and kindly wizards as well as cruel magicians, and if you run afoul of one you go to the other.

It happened, as some people tell it, that a truly evil and malignant witch once cast a spell on a beautiful princess in a distant country, and kept her imprisoned in a castle on a hill for some seven years. She kept a close eye on the wretched princess, guarding against escape, while her young lover, a handsome prince who wanted to save her, wandered hopelessly around the castle hill, looking up sadly at the windows of her tower, where she spent hours in fear, tears and longing. He often wept bitter tears of his own until a certain kindly sorcerer asked what was the matter.

"Don't worry," he told the prince when he heard the story. "I can save her for you. Go home and wait for your princess there, because escape is something she must do alone, or she'll never be free of the witch's spell."

With this, the sorcerer turned into a dove, flew up to the castle, and perched on the imprisoned girl's window sill.

"Here," he said, "is a comb, a brush, an apple and a sheet. Escape from the castle. If the witch comes flying after you, throw down the comb, look once over your shoulder, and then keep on running. If she is still behind you, throw down the brush, look twice behind you, and run on as fast as you can, then look back three times and throw down the apple if she is still coming. If, after that, she is still behind you, throw down the bedsheet, don't look back at all, and run all the way to your father's home."

The princess thanked the kindly dove, repeated his instructions, and settled down to wait for the day when she'd be able to escape from the castle and do what he said.

It happened that the witch flew to Bald Mountain for her witches' frolics on each first Thursday after the new moon and the princess would be left unguarded between dawn and sunset. The reason she had never escaped before was that the witch could always find her if she hid or catch her if she ran. But now, as soon as the witch climbed astride her shovel on the proper day, and got ready to fly to her demon lover, the princess gathered up what the dove had brought her and waited by the gate.

"Bound or Free!" cried the witch. "Devil carry me!"

The shovel zoomed into the air just before the sunrise and vanished in the twilight and the princess slipped out of the gate and ran down the mountain. She ran as quickly as she could, but when she looked back, she saw the witch galloping close behind her on an enormous rooster. It seemed that she hadn't fooled the witch after all, and that she'd be caught at almost any moment.

She tossed the comb behind her, looked back and saw it twisting and winding like a snake until it turned into a long, wide river. The rising sun lit up the broad, blue waters where wild geese and ducks splashed around in flocks, and where the skimming swallows dipped their little wings. The witch, stopped in her tracks by the sudden torrent, boiled with fury on the other shore as she watched the princess running beyond her reach. She jumped back on her rooster, forced it into the water, swam it across the mile-wide river, and started catching up with her prey again.

Tired and pale with fear, the princess threw the brush behind her, glanced back twice, and saw that each bristle had turned into a giant tree, so that a vast, black forest had sprung up in the witch's path, full of thorns and brambles, and packs of wolves started to howl in it. It took the witch a whole day to push her way through the tangled thickets, gorges and ravines, before she could pick up the chase again.

But now the princess was very tired, having run on and on since early Thursday morning, and she couldn't struggle on as quickly as before. She threw down the apple and watched it roll behind her, and then looked back three times to see a vast, steep mountain rising from the apple, with the evil witch trapped on the other side. Foaming with fury at this new obstacle before her, the witch clambered up the rocky slopes for more than a day, and saw from the summit that the fleeing princess, worn and exhausted though she was, was still managing to run in the plain below.

Howling with rage, the witch jumped back on her tired rooster, flew off the mountain, and was just about to seize the poor, running girl by the hem of her dress, when the gasping princess threw the bedsheet back over her shoulder.

She didn't look back, just as the dove had told her, so she didn't see this,

but people who were there say that the wide sheet turned into a wild and even wider ocean, with waves as big as mountains running over it. The witch plunged into it on her panting and exhausted rooster, riding through the waves in a howling gale, and looking like a small mound of snow splashed with boiling foam.

With the last of her strength the escaping princess reached her father's castle. Her lover was there. Her father gave a great feast for the entire country and announced her wedding, and a few days later the castle shined with lights and echoed with music as the brave girl married the young man she loved.

The witch had never managed to cross the great ocean. Her rooster drowned. All her powers failed her. She sat in the wild sea astride her dead rooster, saw the bright lights and listened to the music of the merry dances, and heard the happy shouts of all the guests and the wedding party. She cursed the sea, the winds and everything around her until she burst with rage and that was her end.

The great ocean disappeared the moment she was dead, leaving her body in the castle's pasture, but the wolves and ravens fled from her corpse in fear. People tried to bury her time and time again but the earth refused to keep her unclean bones and threw them out into the open each time she was buried.

At last, one stormy night, a gale swept her evil remnants high into the air and carried them to the castle in which she'd kept the princess. There, scattered in the courtyard in the rain and weather, her dead bones groan and wail on the first Thursday after each new moon, and if you don't believe it you can go and hear it for yourself.

How a Fool Learned the Meaning of Fear

THERE'S AN OLD SAYING that fools rush in where angels fear to tread, but sometimes it's the fear that is foolish while simple courage, innocence and a clear conscience can lead to good fortune.

To make a point, there were once two brothers named Pawel and Gawel, neither smart nor stupid. Pawel thought just what everyone else was thinking, no more and no less; he never came up with a new idea or a different way of looking at life and the world. But Pawel had the reputation of being the smarter because everybody could agree with him.

Gawel was an oddball, too stupid to be human, and the reason everyone called him such a fool was that he didn't understand the meaning of fear. Whenever he heard Pawel saying he was afraid of something, or telling how at one time or another he felt the touch of fear, Gawel could never understand what he was talking about.

"Where did it touch you?" he'd ask. "Did it hurt? Did it burn? Was it hot or cold? What does it look like? Is it big or small? Does it walk, run or crawl? Does it have teeth and claws? Does it have a tail? Does it have two eyes or one? Can you eat it, or does it eat you?"

Fed up with this, and bored with being pestered for explanations of something as obvious as fear, Pawel decided to teach Gawel a lesson he wouldn't soon forget, and he soon got the chance.

It happened that one dark, rainy autumn night their father sent the family fool to the tavern to bring home a bottle of vodka. Pawel knew that Gawel would take a shortcut through the graveyard, so he sneaked out of the cottage, blackened his face with soot, draped his head with his mother's old red skirt, placed a glowing ember in his teeth, and waited for Gawel on the narrow path that wound among the graves.

In a short while Gawel came along, whistling and tossing his cudgel in the air. He'd also tossed down a few drinks while waiting in the tavern and he was feeling quite pleased with himself.

153

"Hey you!" he shouted from a distance, catching sight of someone who blocked his path among the muddy graves. "You with the light in your mouth! Get out of the way, 'cause I'm not going to get my boots muddy just because of you."

But Pawel only groaned as horribly as he could and stayed where he was.

"Are you deaf or what?" Gawel shouted, coming closer to him. "Out of my way, or I'll smack you so hard your teeth will catch fire!"

The clever Pawel thought that in the end even his dimwit brother would panic and run from a ghoul, which is what everybody else would think and do; so he spread his arms wide like an apparition, groaned more horribly than ever, and advanced on Gawel. But because Gawel couldn't grasp the idea of fear he was simply fearless. He hurled himself at the ghost, whacked him across the skull with his thick, oak cudgel, and then kicked, punched, whaled and beat him up so thoroughly that even a real ghoul would've had enough.

Poor Pawel swallowed the hot ember, burned his mouth and gullet, howled like a real lost soul in the Devil's cauldron, got entangled in the red skirt when he tried to run, fell headlong in the mud and finally managed to spit out the coal so that Gawel could tell who he was.

"Is that you, Pawel?" he cried out, amazed. "Hey, I'm real sorry! I didn't know it was you! I mean, how could I? Who'd think that a smart fellow like you would stand in the middle of a graveyard in the rain, with a skirt wrapped around his head and a coal in his mouth? Why would you do something that stupid?"

Snarling and gnashing his teeth with anger and pain, Pawel managed to drag himself home. But his father flew into a rage when he saw what happened to his clever son. He seized a bull whip, and he'd have taken all the hide off Gawel's back, if the fearless fool hadn't climbed into the hayloft and pulled up the ladder after him.

Next day, however, Pawel was too sick to get out of bed. The local leech had to be called to bleed him and set cupping glasses on his back. This, and the money that he had to spend, so enraged his father that he threw Gawel out of the house to shift for himself until pain, poverty and hunger taught him the meaning of fear. His mother (who like all the mothers, loved her stupid son even more than she cared for the clever one) begged that he be given one more chance, but the furious father wouldn't change his mind.

"A real man doesn't change his mind!" he shouted. "Everybody knows that. And until this fool learns to think like everybody else I don't want to see him!"

So poor Gawel left, taking along all of his belongings and a small pouch of copper coins that his mother slipped into his pocket.

A week later, after wandering about without any particular direction, he stopped in a tavern. It was market day and the tavern was full of peasants, shouting, joking, singing and drinking up their profits before they went home. But when they asked him who he was, where he was bound, and why he was on the road, Gawel was stumped for an answer they would understand.

"My name is Gawel," he said honestly. "That much I'm sure about. As for where I'm going, and why I'm on the road, all I can say is that I'm looking for fear."

Everyone burst out laughing, not sure if this was stupidity or wit, and the innkeeper slapped him on the back.

"Well," he said. "If that's all you're looking for, you'll find it right here. D'you see that huge castle up on the hill? God only knows how long it's been empty but nobody wants to live there because of the ghosts. Go sleep there if you want a taste of fear. You'll get enough to last you a lifetime!"

"Really?" Gawel cried, delighted. "Listen, I'd be glad to pay for this tip if I get to understand what fear is about! But I don't think that's going to happen. Just give me plenty to eat and drink because I'll get bored sitting there all night."

When everybody realized that he was dead serious, and that he really meant to spend the night in the haunted castle, they got worried at once.

"Hey," said the innkeeper, "You'd better think that over. A lot of fine fellows went up there on a bet and not one of 'em ever came back again."

"Don't be a fool!" cried another man. "Don't stake your young life on a thing like that!"

But the more they argued and pleaded with Gawel, the more pleased he was that he'd finally look fear in the face. Nobody thought he'd live through this trial by terror — after all, nobody did before — and when they couldn't scare him out of the idea, they tried to make his last hours on earth as comfortable as they could. Before nightfall, they carted enough logs and kindling to the castle to last until morning. They also loaded Gawel with garlands of sausage, strings of liverwurst, a huge bowl of potatoes cooked with bacon and savory lumps of fatback, and one or two flasks of vodka. Then they took Gawel to the haunted castle and bid him goodbye.

Alone in the castle, Gawel settled in for a long night of waiting. He lit a fire in the fireplace of the biggest chamber. He dragged a huge table and a chair to the fire, put up his feet, lit a pipe, and listened to the mournful howling of the wind in the great stone chimney. Anyone else's hair might have stood on end at this ghostly sound but Gawel only thought that it was kind of pretty. From time to time he sipped a little vodka and finally he got hungry. He put his pot of bacon and potatoes on the fire, spitted some sausage on an old sword he found lying there, and started cooking himself a supper.

But he no sooner did that when a glum, gloomy voice echoed down the chimney.

"I'm coming down!" it cried.

"Hey, hang on a bit!" Gawel shouted up. "What about my supper? I just got the spuds to boil and the sausage isn't even brown!"

But the grim, ghostly voice only cried again: "I am coming down!"

"Right in the middle of my supper," Gawel growled. "If that's fear I don't think I'll like it." Then he removed his potato pot and the spitted sausage, put them on the table, and shouted up to the unseen above him: "Come on down if you want to, though I don't care where you go!"

Something came banging and rattling down the chimney and one half of a human carcass — from the waist down to the huge, splayed feet — landed on the coals. Annoyed, Gawel reached in and grabbed it by one foot and hurled it over his shoulder. He was about to put his supper back on the fire again when the deep, ghostly voice boomed once more down the chimney:

"I am coming down!"

"To the Devil with this fear!" Gawel cursed. "Looks like I won't even get my dinner cooked." And to the unseen and unknown he shouted: "Go where you want and to the Devil with you!"

This time the top half of a man fell into the fire, along with a horrible cruel face, a bushy beard, and mad rolling eyes. Gawel tossed this where he threw the other. He waited a while to see if any other bits and pieces would come down the chimney, then put his potato pot back on the boil and hung his spitted sausage over the coals.

"Anything else flying down," he shouted, "or is this the lot?"

But nothing more came tumbling into the fireplace. So he cooked his supper in peace, dumped it into a bowl, and set it on the table. But suddenly, as he swung around for something, he saw a huge, lowering apparition, with blood-red eyes and wild beard and hair, erect and reassembled right behind his chair.

"Hey, friend," he called out cheerfully, "what're you standing there for like a stump in a cornfield? Sit down and have a bite! I don't like to eat alone and have people staring down my gullet."

The frightful apparition seized a chair and sat down but it didn't eat.

"Help yourself, why don't you? There's enough for a dozen here," Gawel urged the ghost with almost every bite. But when the ghoul refused his invitations he shrugged and finished off all the food himself.

When he had only one last bite of sausage left, however, the ghost said: "Gimme that."

"Forget it," said Gawel. "You wouldn't eat when I asked you to, so now suck your thumb."

"What!" the ghoul howled. "You're not afraid of me? You don't understanding the meaning of fear?"

"Oh come on," Gawel said. "What's all this fear business? My smart brother Pawel keeps talking about fear. But where is it? What's it all about? And how come everybody talks about it as if it was real? Seems to me it's just something everybody invents for himself and then gets mad if nobody else believes him."

At this the dreadful apparition burst into grateful tears.

"Thank you, oh thank you!" it cried. "You've just saved me from torments I've been enduring for 100 years. I used to be the lord here. I ruled by blood and terror. Whoever stood up to me I seized and sawed in half with a gap-toothed saw. Now demons saw me in half every night. They turned me into the name and meaning of fear around here. And they'd keep doing it for all eternity if you hadn't laughed at me, stood up to me, and refused to feed me. Once you feed fear you're as good as finished, and I'd have torn you apart in a flash if you'd let me have that last bit of sausage. But you looked fear in the eye the way it should be looked at and now I am free."

"Fine," Gawel said. "So what will you give me?"

"Such treasures as will strike you blind," said the apparition and led Gawel down many winding stairs to a secret dungeon.

And what a hoard that was! The loot of the ages! The gold and jewels and silverplate and art-works cast such a brilliant light that it was hard to see anything within it. Many brave fellows were blinded by it, the ghost said, and stumbled around in the treasure until they dropped dead, but Gawel couldn't see anything the way everybody else looked at it. To him light was light, like jewels were jewels, and he picked the costliest since the ghost told him he could carry out anything he wanted.

"Maybe I'm stupid," he said. "My smart brother Pawel would probably know exactly what to go for, but what do I know? So all I'll take is every diamond the size of a goose egg and be content with that."

That's what he did. But he learned something else about the world, and people, during this adventure.

When he got back to the inn he said that yes, the ghost had scared the stuffing out of him, and beaten the living daylights out of him just as it did everybody else, so that he'd barely escaped with his life. He'd promised the innkeeper something for his tip but, under the circumstances, nobody was surprised when he gave him nothing. He just hired a wagon to take him to the city.

A few months later those who heard about it were surprised to learn that Gawel was a great lord, married to a countess. He became famous in the country as Gawel the Smart who gave the most sought-after dinners in the capital, who seemed to think and do what everyone else seemed to think and do, and who never questioned the meaning of fear.

Where Devils Are Helpless

PEOPLE SAY THAT LOVE, tranquility and hard work is the glue that holds marriages together, and that's the one thing that can make the Devil jump into holy water. They go mad when they can't get a loving couple suspecting each other, yelling at each other, and throwing each other out of the house. Fortunately for them that's never happened in a marriage since men and women started to live together, but there can always be a first time and the Devil knows it.

It happened that there was once an old man and woman who spent a whole lifetime together without a cross word or a sidelong glance. They worked side by side in the fields, shared all their joys and troubles, and they were so devoted to each other that each thought only of how to make the other happy. The Devil tried every trick in his book to set them at odds but nothing seemed to work.

And he tried everything. He sent a young witch, disguised as a milk-maid, to tempt the old man. He gave a rich husband to the woman's sister so that she'd be envious and then dissatisfied with her own. He even scorched their crops one hot summer so that they'd be poor, since it's well known that grinding poverty starves love in marriage faster than a famine. But the old man had eyes only for his wife, and bored the young witch to death with his constant praises of his loving woman. The wife, instead of envying her sister, felt truly sorry for her because her rich husband was a cheat who shortchanged the people and clipped the silver with which he bought their harvests.

It seemed to the desperate Devil that he'd become the first demon who failed to wreck a marriage, and turn into the laughing stock of hell.

"What's gone wrong?" he howled at night in the forest. "Have I lost my touch? If this goes on much longer I'll have to turn into a sexton and ring bells on Sundays."

159

Mad with rage, and sick about the end of his career, the Devil rammed his head against a tree, twisted his horns backwards, gnawed on his own tail, got as thin a rail and dried up like a piece of kindling. But nothing worked. He couldn't come up with a single deviltry that would do the trick. At last, as heartbroken as a heartless devil gets to be and ready to give up, he took a long sad walk around the village, his head and horns hung low on his chest and his tail dragging.

But suddenly he met the old couple's neighbor, a dried up old prune with a face the color of smoked fish, and with sharp little pebble eyes that peered everywhere at once. Some people thought she was a witch, and even tried to drown her a few times in the village pond, but she always bobbed up to the surface and never touched bottom. She was, however, the biggest and most spiteful gossip in the county, never happy, as the saying goes, 'until she got somebody on the edge of her tongue,' and she took one look at the gloomy Devil and cackled with malice.

"What's wrong with you, my friend?" she croaked while her beady eyes glittered in anticipation. "Did you get a whiff of incense near the church, or did somebody poke you with an aspen stake?"

"I wish that's all it was," groaned the helpless Devil. "One can get over a beating even with an aspen, and a good sneezing will clean the nose of incense. But when you twist yourself inside out to corrupt somebody, and they just get better, that's real despair."

"Who's such a saint around here, then?" the old hag licked her lips, smelling a chance for gossip.

"Who but your neighbors?" And the Devil told her the whole story.

"Hee hee hee!" she laughed. "Is that all? You can't be much of a Devil, my lad, if they're too much for you. So you didn't trip them up today, so what? You'll get them tomorrow. Nobody loves anybody else for ever, that's just human nature. Sooner or later something will go wrong. What are they, turtledoves? Come on, snap out of it, get your horns on straight, there are pills for all ills, ask any old gossip. All couples quarrel, get suspicious and yell at each other; you just have to give them a push with a word or two."

"What word?" cried the Devil. "I've used up all the words I knew and a few I've stolen and I can't put a dent in that love of theirs! I'll have to drown myself in holy water if this goes on much longer!"

"Pshaw!" the old gossip snorted with contempt. "I don't know what's happened to Devils anymore! Giving up this easy! If you can't peer through the door, you peek through the window, you know the old saying. If you can't get anywhere with him, take a shot at her. Huh! I could have 'em fighting like wild dogs over a marrow bone before the day's over."

"Take mercy on me, Granny," the Devil begged, "or I'll have to hang myself on my own tail. Do your worst! Get them to hate each other! You do that and I'll give you anything you want."

"Will you give me a new pair of shoes?" she asked, although a real gossip, the kind that lived among us even before there were any Devils, will do harm just for the pleasure of it.

"You can have a dozen!"

"One pair's enough," she grinned. "I only have two feet. Go fetch the shoes and I'll have your two old turtledoves snarling before nightfall."

The Devil bounded off to get the woman's shoes, and she trotted to her neighbor's field where the old man was just finishing his work.

"So what's new?" she asked. "How's everything going?"

"Couldn't be better," the good man replied. "There's always one thing or another, that goes without saying, but with a woman as good as mine even a year in hell would feel like a day in heaven. And how're things with you?"

"Not so good," she croaked. "I worry about you, neighbor. You're such a good man you don't see the evil right under your nose, and that's the worst kind. I'd be the last to cause you any trouble, but I've got to warn you that you're in for a shock tonight."

"What shock, for Godssake!" cried the man. "What kind of trouble?"

"Well, it's your wife," she muttered, "though I'd tear my tongue out rather than say it to you."

"My wife? What about my wife?"

"Well, she doesn't love you like you think. She's seeing a fellow. I mind my own business, as you know, but I heard them myself plotting to do you in."

"My wife! You're crazy! That's impossible!"

"Maybe I'm wrong," she sighed. "Maybe it's best not to interfere. But what else can I do when your life's in danger?"

"My life?" he shouted. "Who's going to kill me?"

"You'll see for yourself when you get home tonight. Your wife will start stroking your hair straight away. She'll get you to stretch out with your head on her knees and she'll be making like she combs your hair. Well, just watch and see if she doesn't pull a razor from under her apron and try to cut your throat."

"Impossible!" cried the man, but he sat down on a stump the moment the old gossip ran back to the village, and started turning it all over in his mind.

Could it be? Oh, surely, it couldn't! But once a seed of doubt is planted by malicious gossip it'll grow and fester, and the old man began to sigh and wonder, and then two large tears rolled down his face without him even knowing.

Meanwhile the gossip ran to the man's home where she found the wife busy with her mending.

"Good evening, neighbor!" she cried, walking in. "And how are you today?"

"As well as can be," the good wife replied. "And how about you, neighbor?"

"Oh I'm well, as much as anything is well when you're getting old," creaked the village gossip. "But your husband is in real danger!"

"For Godssake!" the wife cried out. "What happened? He was as right as rain when he went out into the fields this morning!"

"Oh, nothing's happened yet, but he'll die tonight," the old hag muttered and faked a sigh of pity. "I see his death as clear as I see you before me."

"Dear God!" cried the wife. "Can't anything be done? I'll be grateful to you all my life, good neighbor, if you'll think of something!"

"Well, yes, there's a way," the old gossip said. "In fact that's why I'm here, to give you some advice. He doesn't know himself that his death is hiding in his hair. You'll probably feel it there yourself if you stroke his head. Get him to stretch out after dinner, put his head in your lap, and find the longest hair on his head. Then get a razor out from under your apron and cut it off at the scalp. That's where his death is hiding. Get rid of it and he'll be just fine. Leave it there and he'll be dead tomorrow."

The poor, frightened wife couldn't wait for her husband to come home for dinner. He too came back from work so worried and unhappy that he looked ready to lie down and die, and she began to stroke his hair at once to see if she could find that death that was hiding there.

"Stretch out here on the bench, my love," she told him after dinner. "Let me comb your hair. Put your head here on my knees and close your eyes a while."

Ah, the poor man thought and wiped away a tear, so the old hag was right. It's all happening like she said it would. He did as his wife asked but he kept his eyes ajar so that he could watch her and saw her pull a razor from under her apron. He leaped off the bench, knocked the razor out of his wife's hands and threw her to the floor.

"Ah!" he yelled. "So that's what you're up to? You'd like to kill me so you can run off with your lover? But I've been warned about you and your lies won't help you anymore!"

The poor wife wept, protesting that she was only trying to save his life, but he wouldn't listen. Suspicion had turned to certainty in his head and nothing could shake it. He beat her until his arm grew numb and then threw her out of his house for ever.

The Devil watched it all, standing invisible right outside their windows, and couldn't believe how easy it had been. He went at once to the old gossip's house to give her the shoes, but on the way he got an idea that would make him the most famous Devil of them all.

"Where the Devil's helpless," he muttered to himself, "just send an old woman. Gossip is stronger than all the powers of hell."